A 4D BOOK

ADVENTURES iN MAKERSPACE

A ROBOTICS MISSION

WRITTEN BY
SHANNON McCLINTOCK MILLER
AND
BLAKE HOENA

ILLUSTRATED BY
ALAN BROWN

STONE ARCH BOOKS
a capstone imprint

capstone®

www.mycapstone.com

A Robotics Mission is published by Stone Arch Books,
a Capstone imprint
1710 Roe Crest Drive, North Mankato, Minnesota 56003
www.mycapstonepub.com

Library of Congress Cataloging-in-Publication Data is available on the Library of Congress website.

ISBN: 978-1-4965-7746-7 (hardcover)
ISBN: 978-1-4965-7750-4 (paperback)
ISBN: 978-1-4965-7754-2 (eBook PDF)

Book design and art direction: Mighty Media
Editorial direction: Kellie M. Hultgren
Music direction: Elizabeth Draper
Music written and produced by Mark Mallman

Printed and bound in the United States of America.
PA017

CONTENTS

Download the Capstone app!

- Ask an adult to download the Capstone 4D app.
- Scan the cover and stars inside the book for additional content.

When you scan a spread, you'll find fun extra stuff to go with this book! You can also find these things on the web at www.capstone4D.com using the password: robot.77467

MEET THE SPECIALIST

ABILITIES:
speed reader, tech titan,
foreign language master,
traveler through literature
and history

MS. GILLIAN
TEACHER-LIBRARIAN

MEET THE STUDENTS

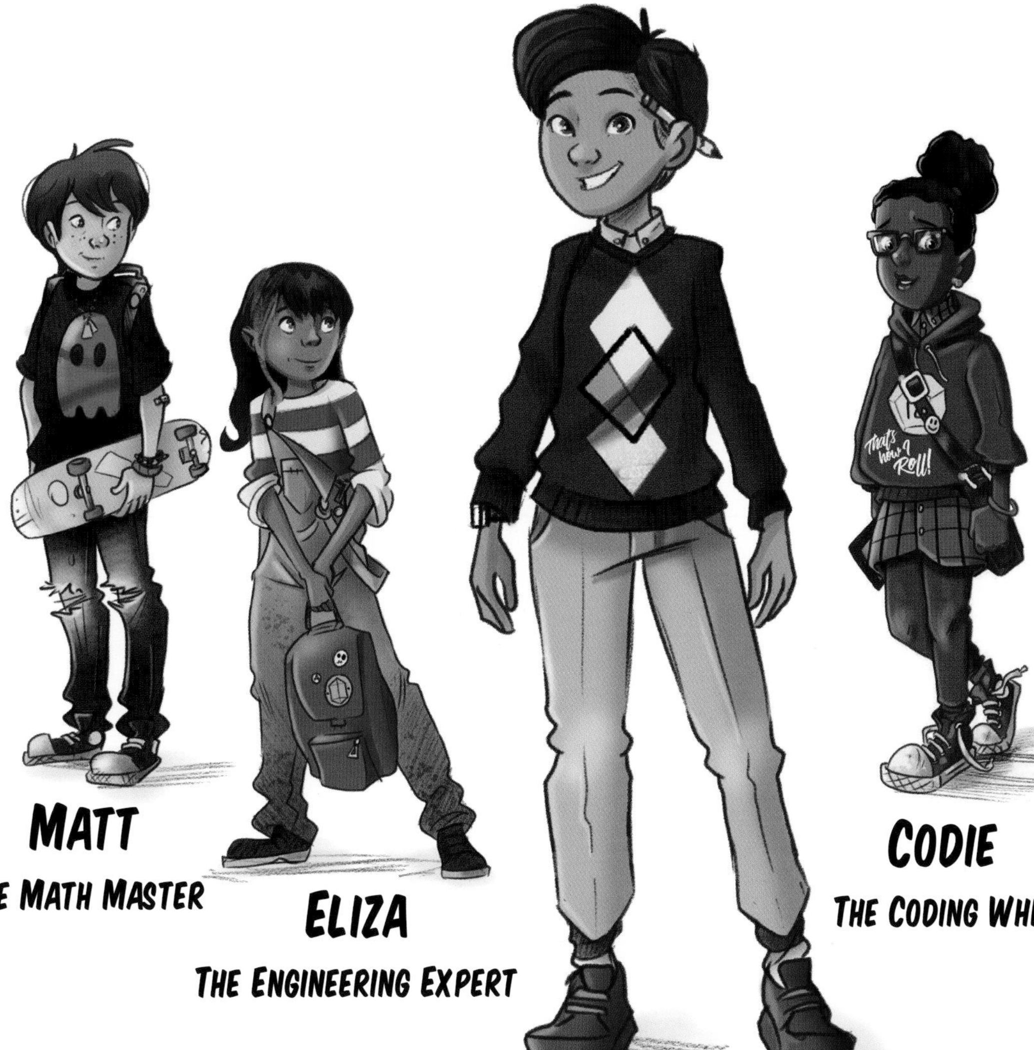
That's how I Roll!

MATT
THE MATH MASTER

ELIZA
THE ENGINEERING EXPERT

CYRUS
THE SCIENCE GENIUS

CODIE
THE CODING WHIZ

BOXES AND BOXES

TODAY, CYRUS AND HIS FRIENDS ARE BRINGING SUPPLIES TO THEIR FAVORITE PLACE IN EMERSON ELEMENTARY. AT THE BACK OF THE SCHOOL'S LIBRARY IS AN AREA THAT MS. GILLIAN CALLS THE MAKERSPACE.

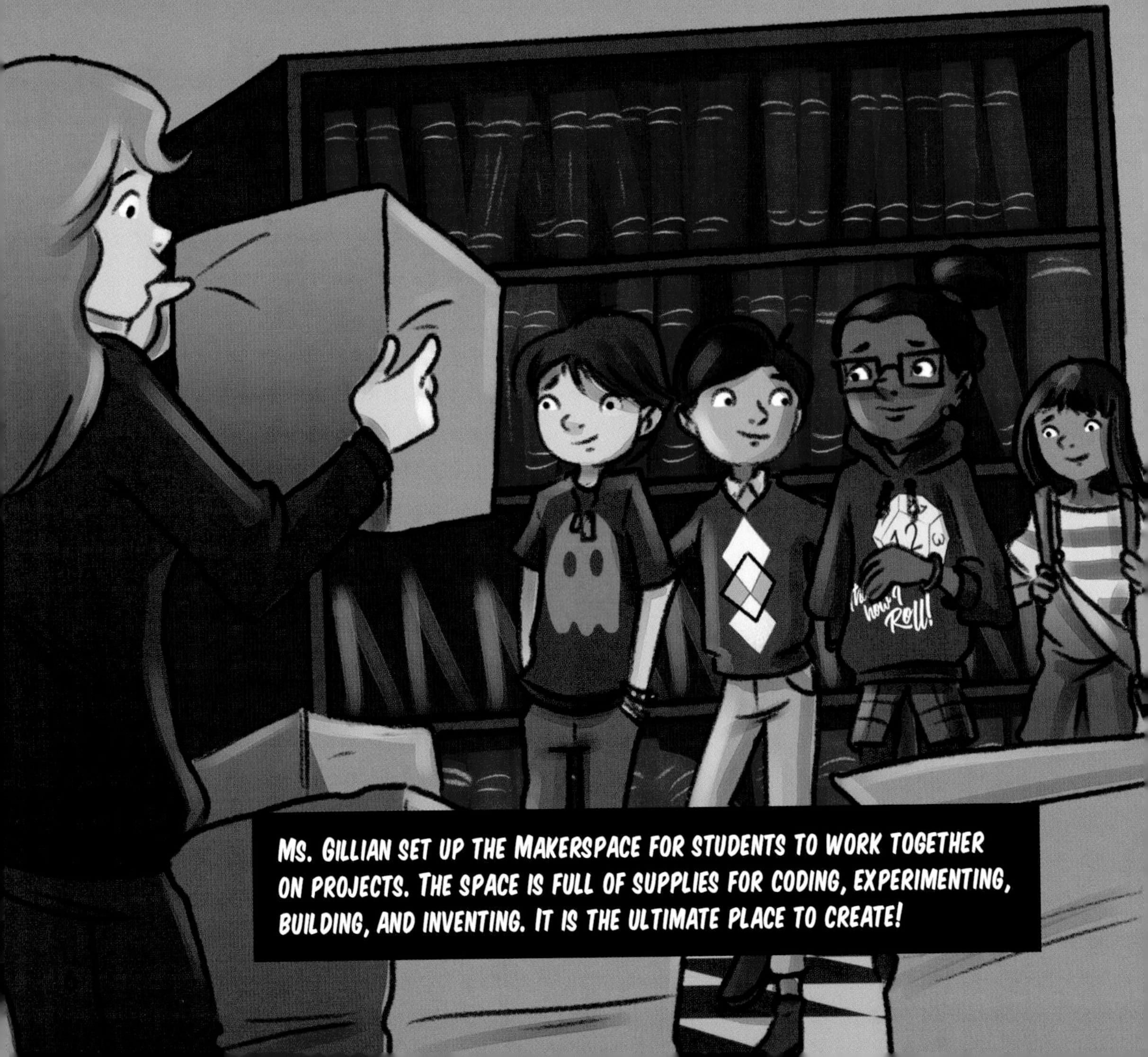
MS. GILLIAN SET UP THE MAKERSPACE FOR STUDENTS TO WORK TOGETHER ON PROJECTS. THE SPACE IS FULL OF SUPPLIES FOR CODING, EXPERIMENTING, BUILDING, AND INVENTING. IT IS THE ULTIMATE PLACE TO CREATE!

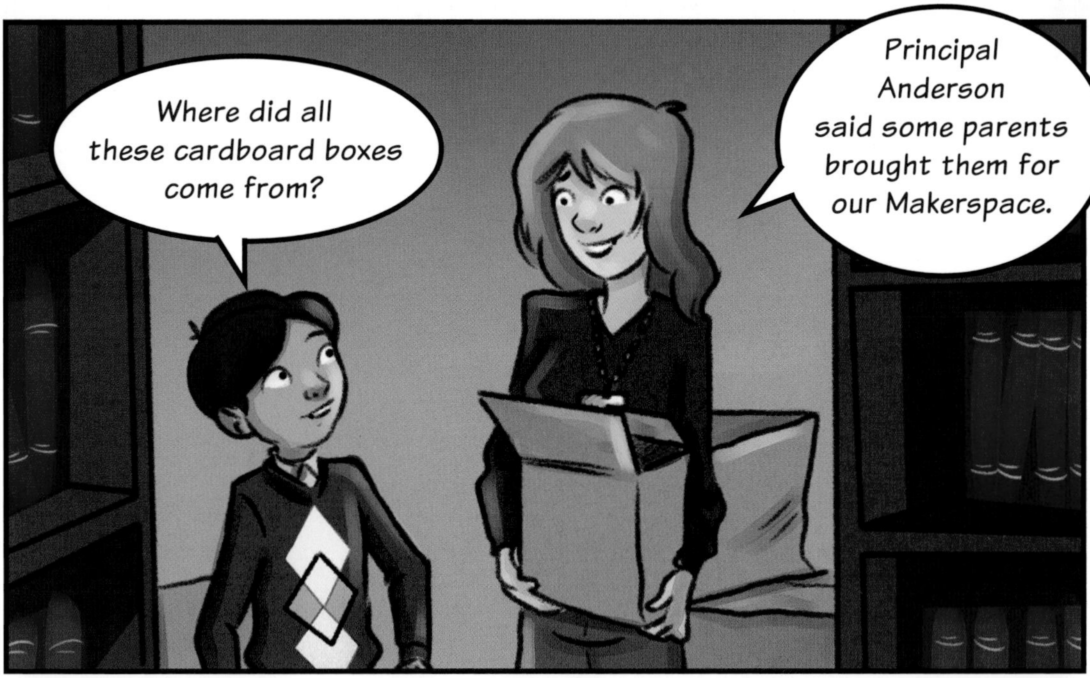
Where did all these cardboard boxes come from?
Principal Anderson said some parents brought them for our Makerspace.

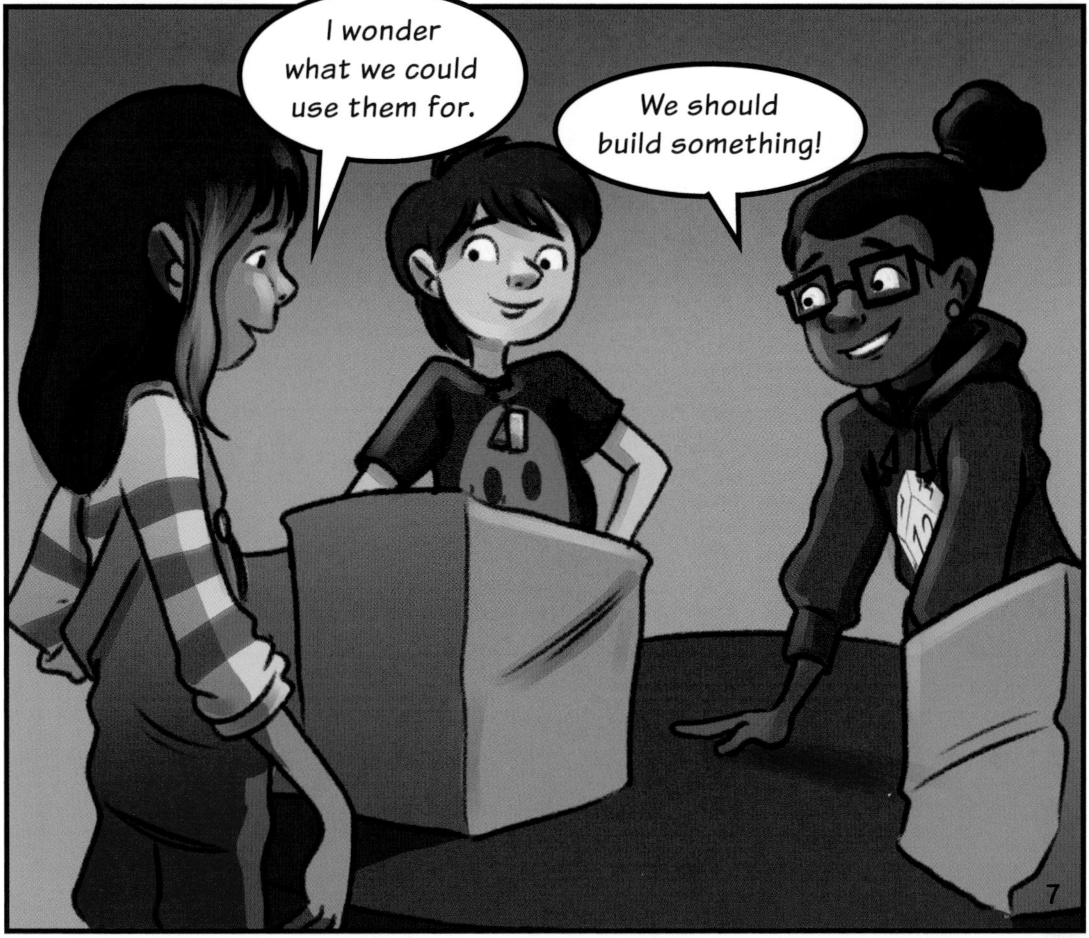
I wonder what we could use them for.
We should build something!

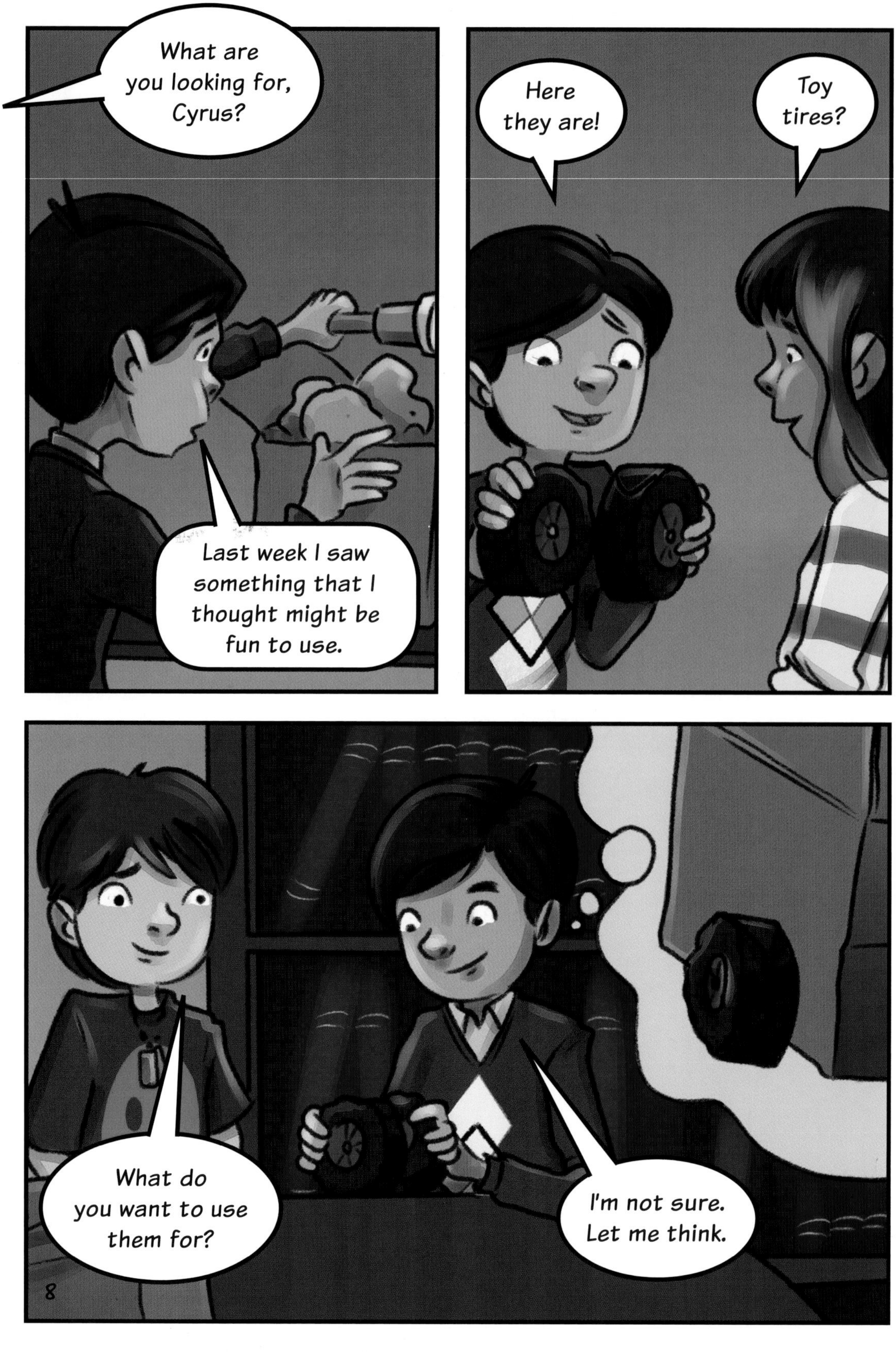
What are you looking for, Cyrus?
Last week I saw something that I thought might be fun to use.
Here they are!
Toy tires?
What do you want to use them for?
I'm not sure. Let me think.

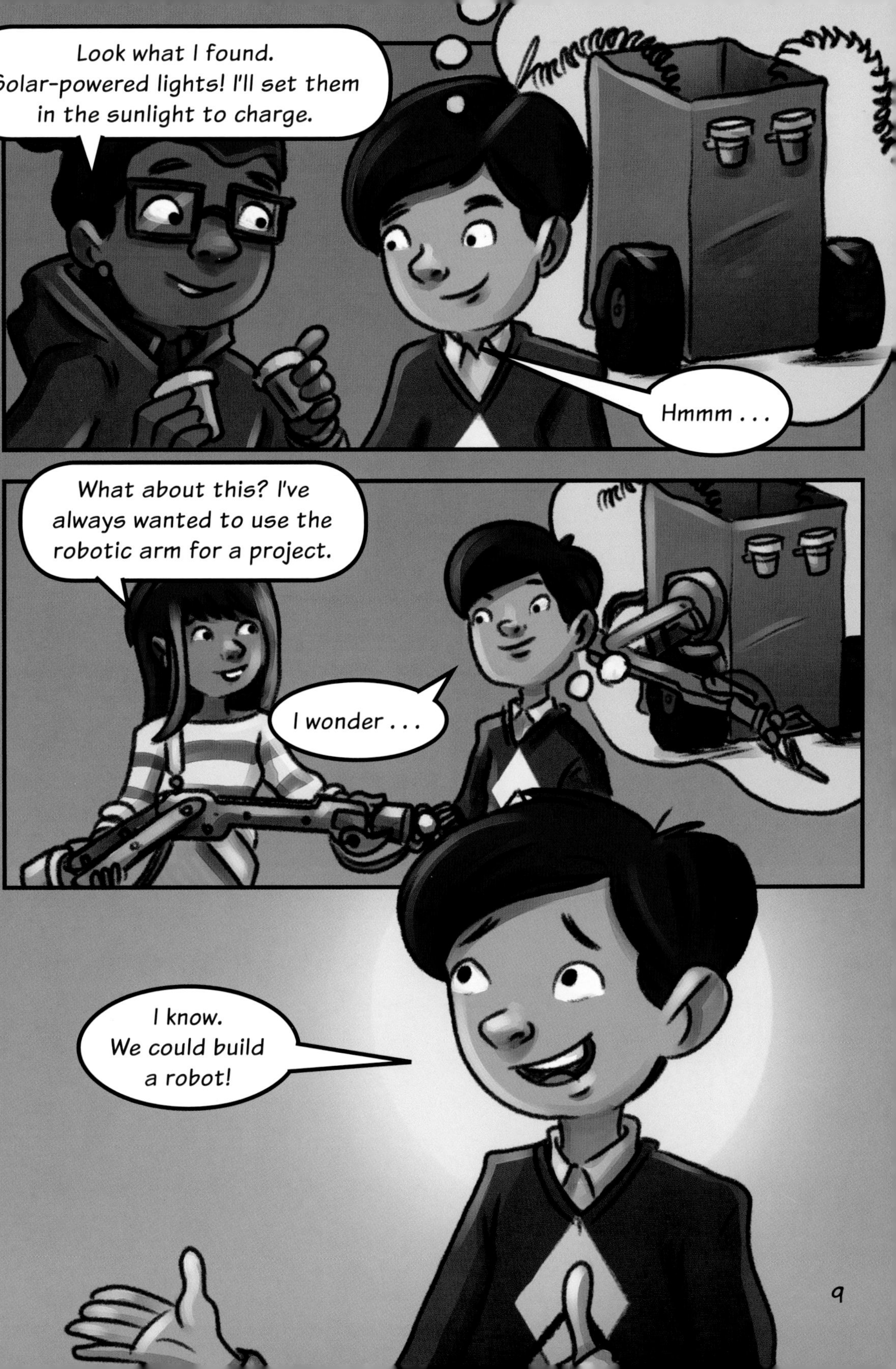

Look what I found. Solar-powered lights! I'll set them in the sunlight to charge.
Hmmm . . .
What about this? I've always wanted to use the robotic arm for a project.
I wonder . . .
I know. We could build a robot!

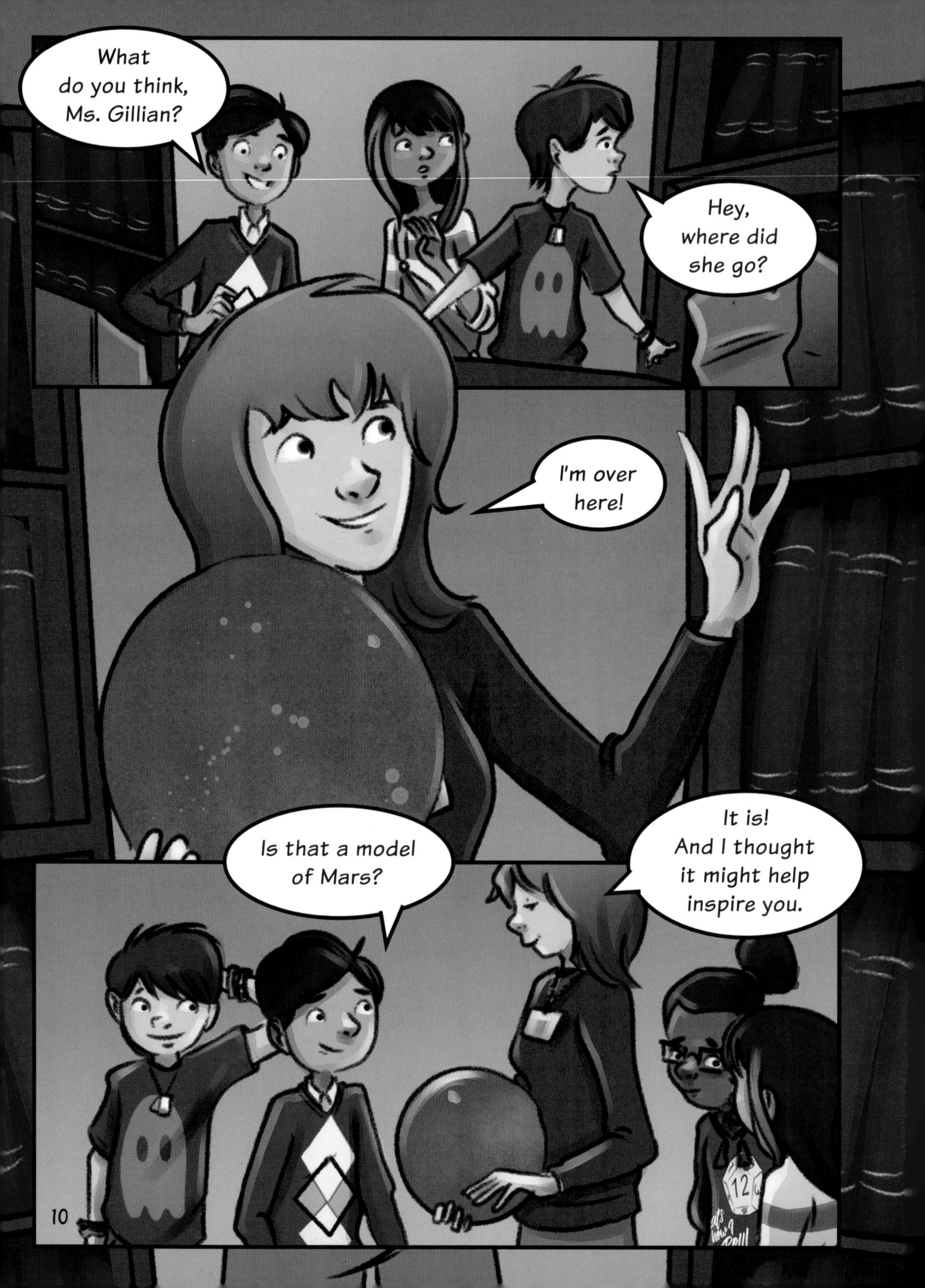
What do you think, Ms. Gillian?
Hey, where did she go?
I'm over here!
Is that a model of Mars?
It is! And I thought it might help inspire you.

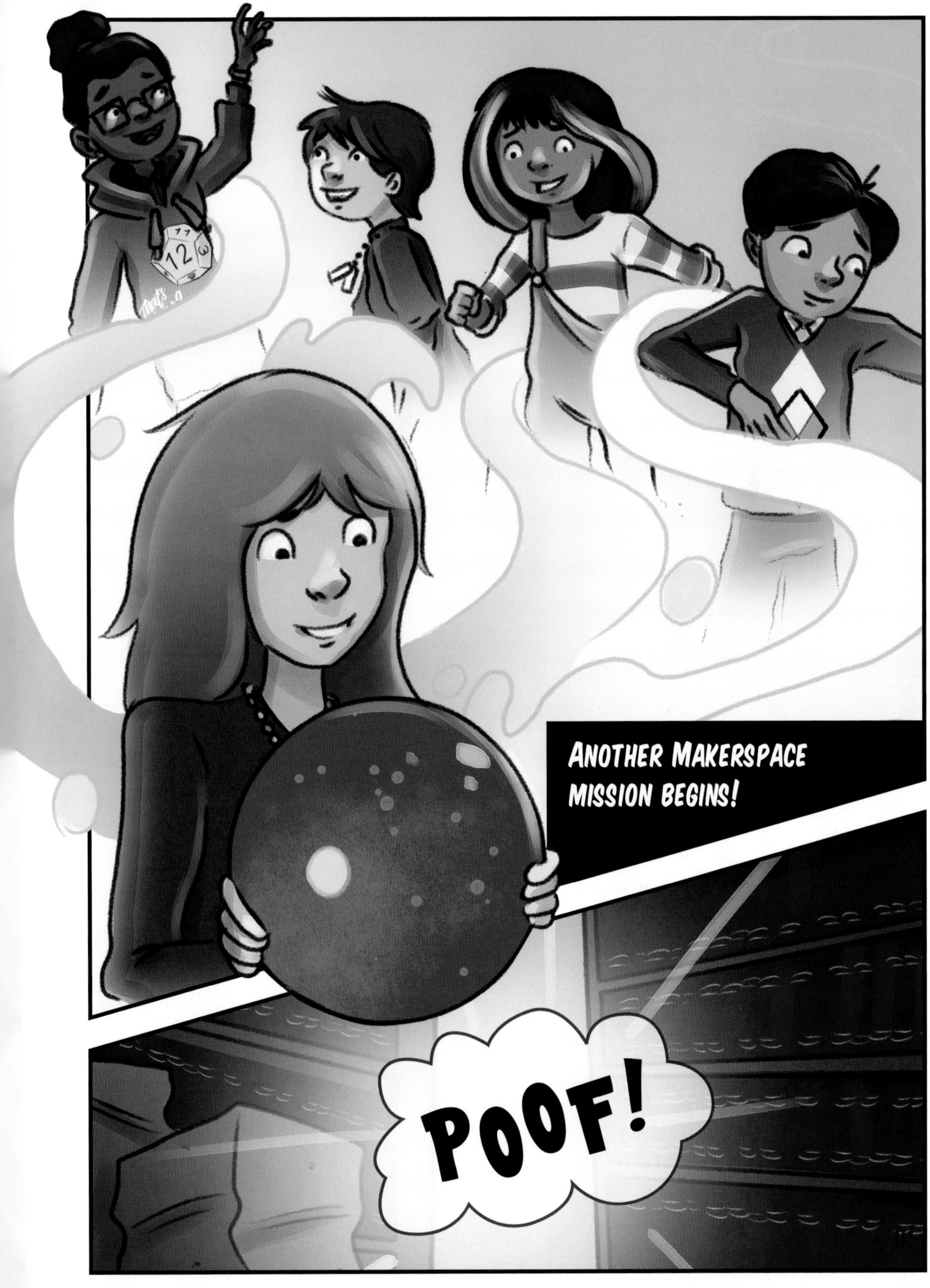
ANOTHER MAKERSPACE MISSION BEGINS!
POOF!

THE RED PLANET

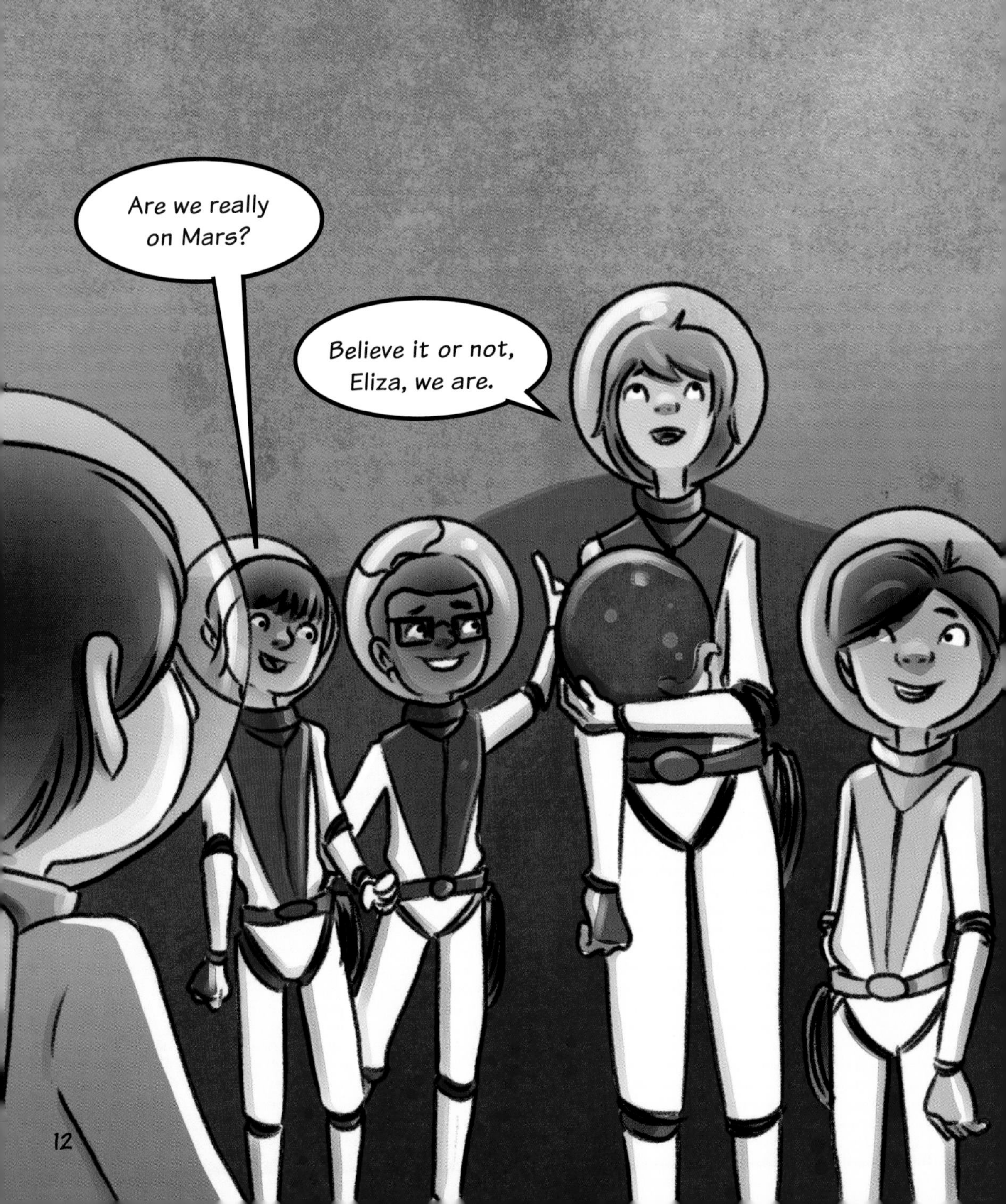
Are we really on Mars?
Believe it or not, Eliza, we are.

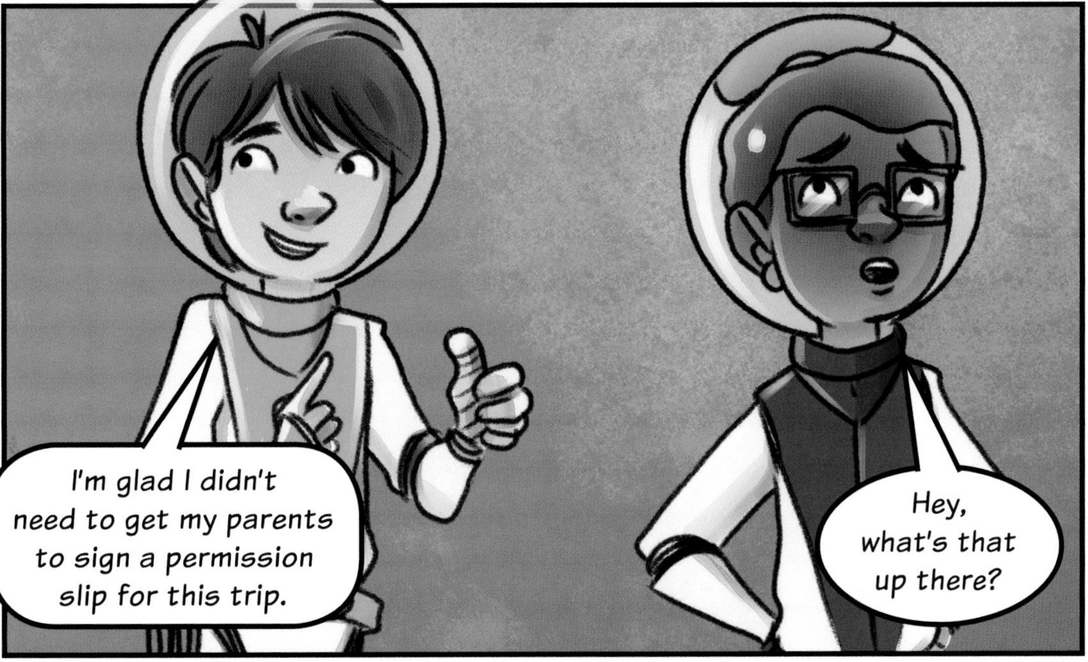
I'm glad I didn't need to get my parents to sign a permission slip for this trip.
Hey, what's that up there?

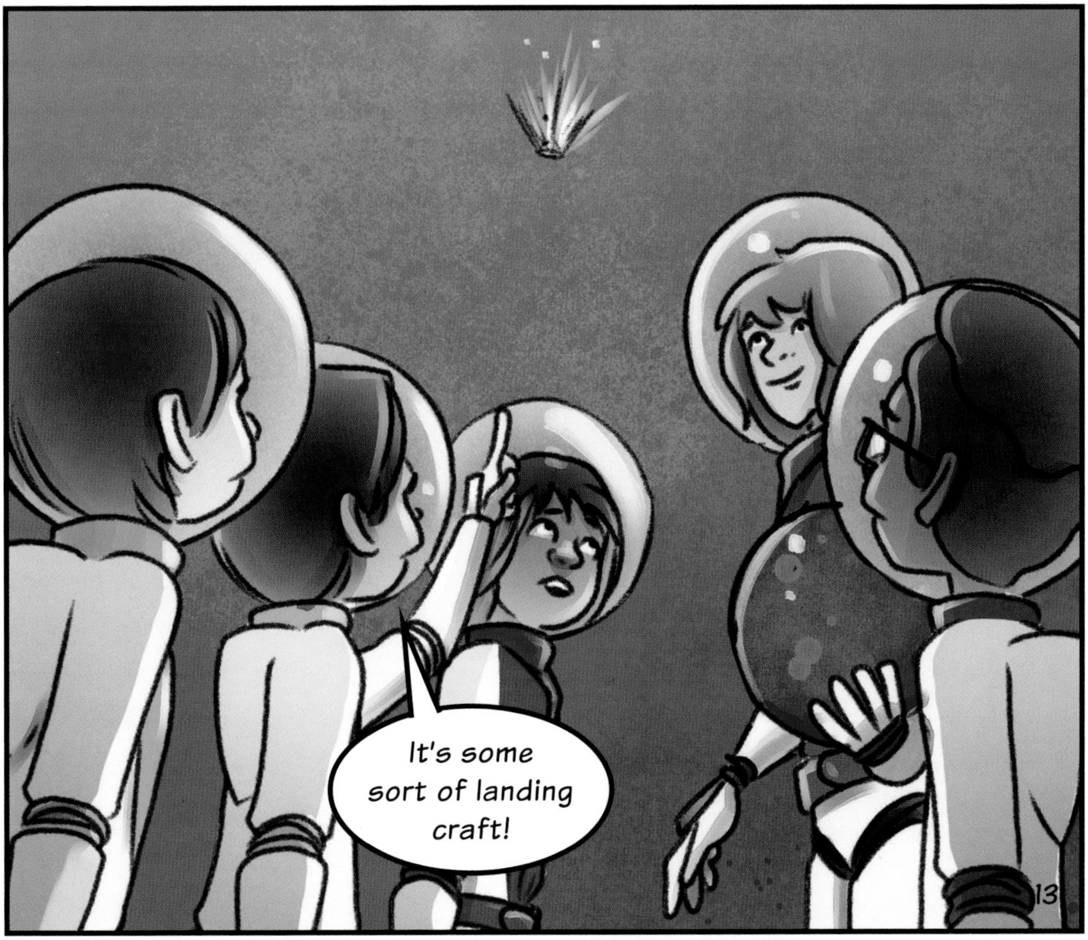
It's some sort of landing craft!

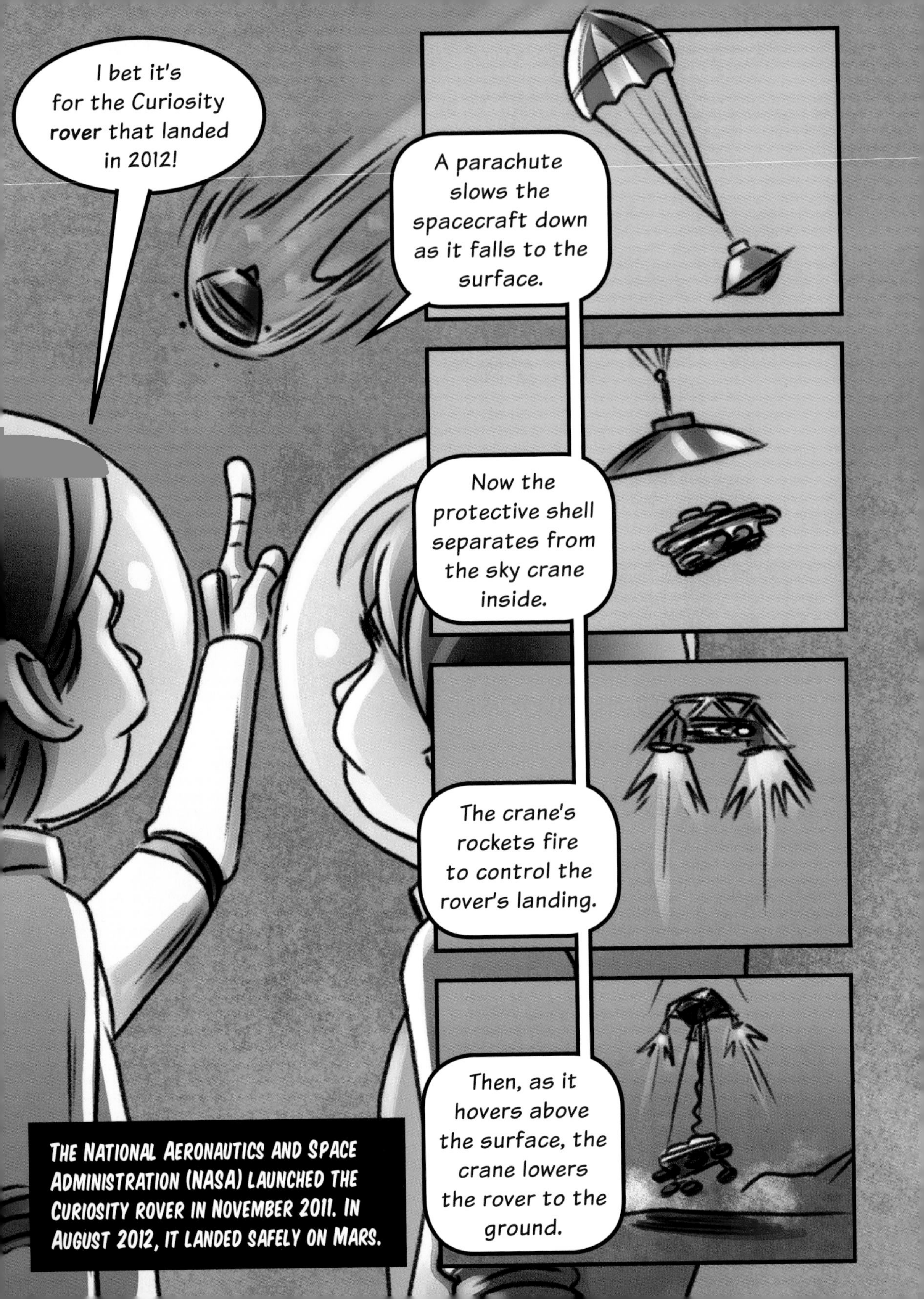
I bet it's for the Curiosity **rover** that landed in 2012!
A parachute slows the spacecraft down as it falls to the surface.
Now the protective shell separates from the sky crane inside.
The crane's rockets fire to control the rover's landing.
Then, as it hovers above the surface, the crane lowers the rover to the ground.
THE NATIONAL AERONAUTICS AND SPACE ADMINISTRATION (NASA) LAUNCHED THE CURIOSITY ROVER IN NOVEMBER 2011. IN AUGUST 2012, IT LANDED SAFELY ON MARS.

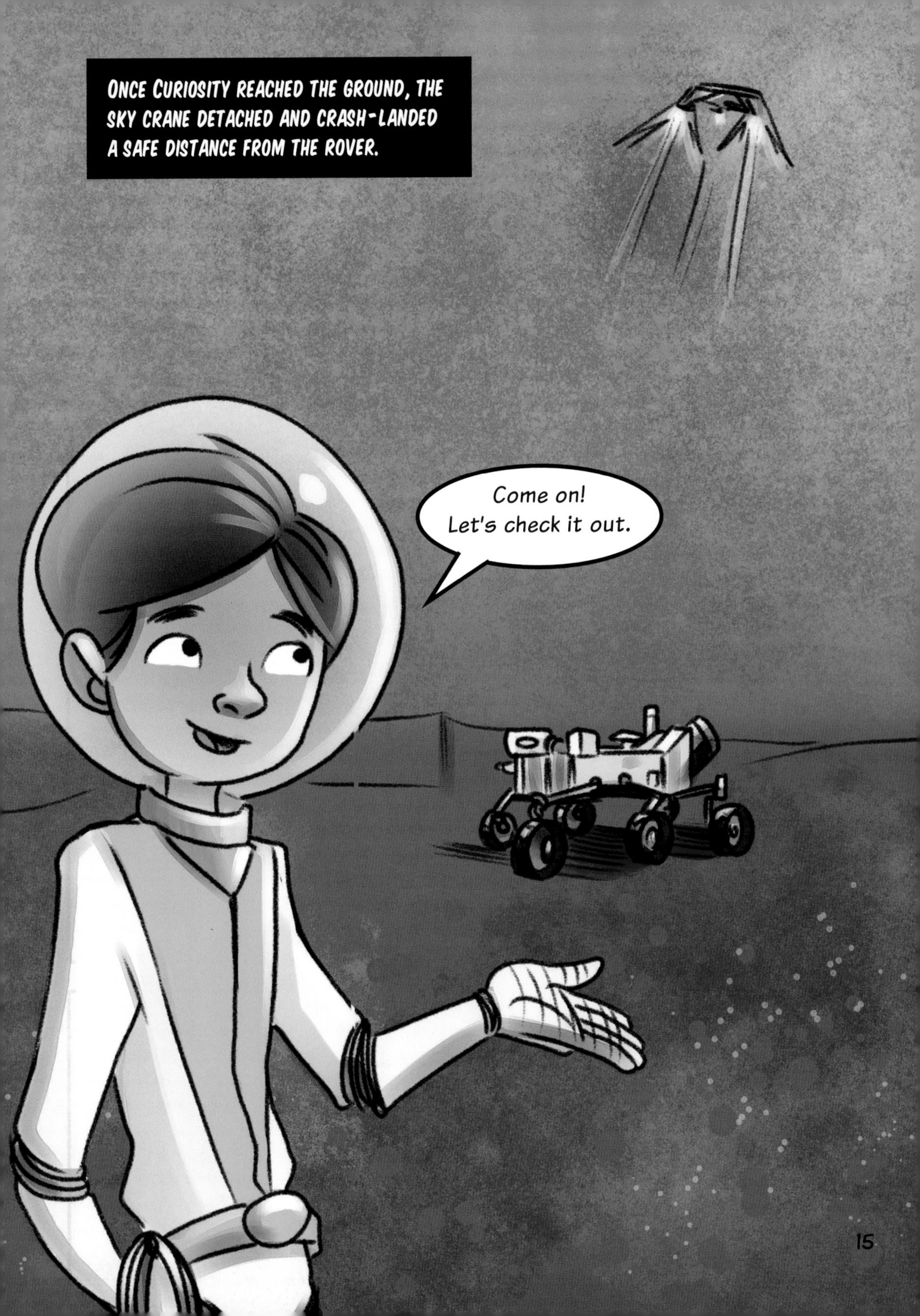
ONCE CURIOSITY REACHED THE GROUND, THE SKY CRANE DETACHED AND CRASH-LANDED A SAFE DISTANCE FROM THE ROVER.
Come on! Let's check it out.

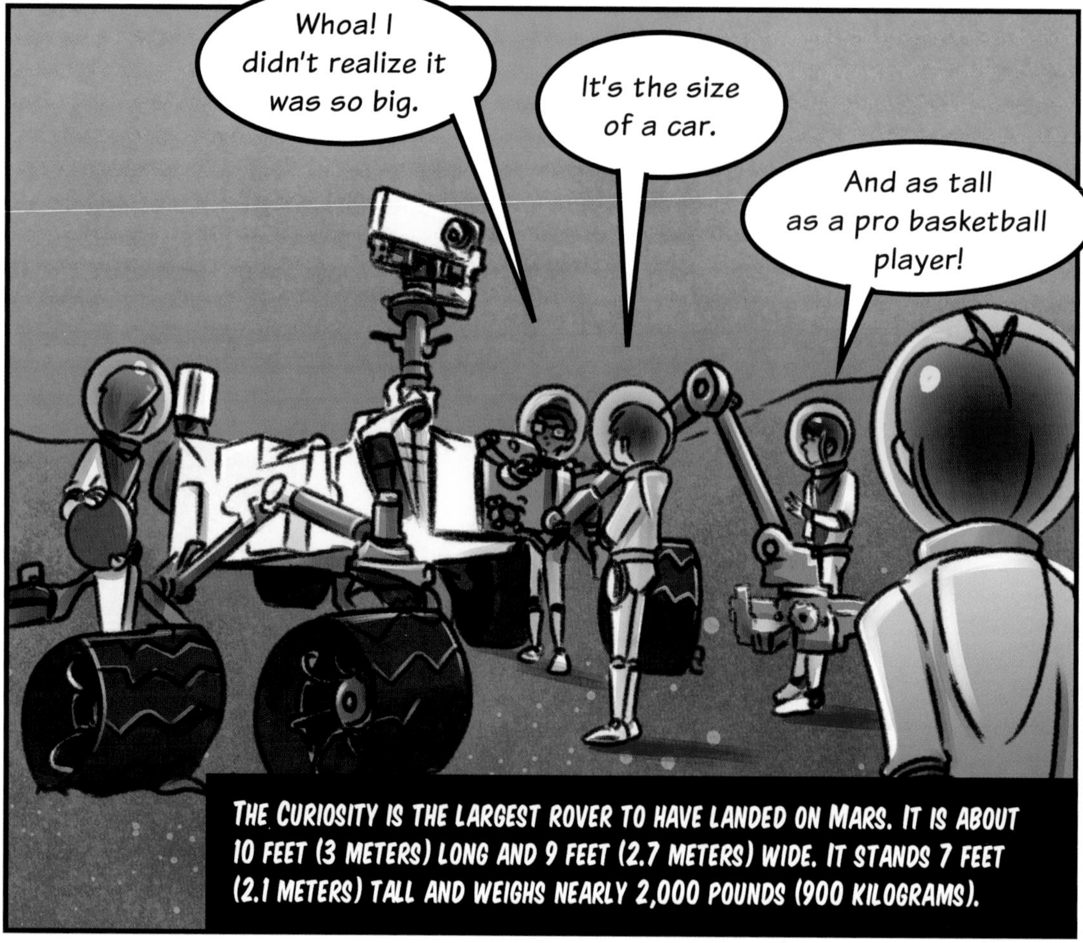
Whoa! I didn't realize it was so big.
It's the size of a car.
And as tall as a pro basketball player!
THE CURIOSITY IS THE LARGEST ROVER TO HAVE LANDED ON MARS. IT IS ABOUT 10 FEET (3 METERS) LONG AND 9 FEET (2.7 METERS) WIDE. IT STANDS 7 FEET (2.1 METERS) TALL AND WEIGHS NEARLY 2,000 POUNDS (900 KILOGRAMS).

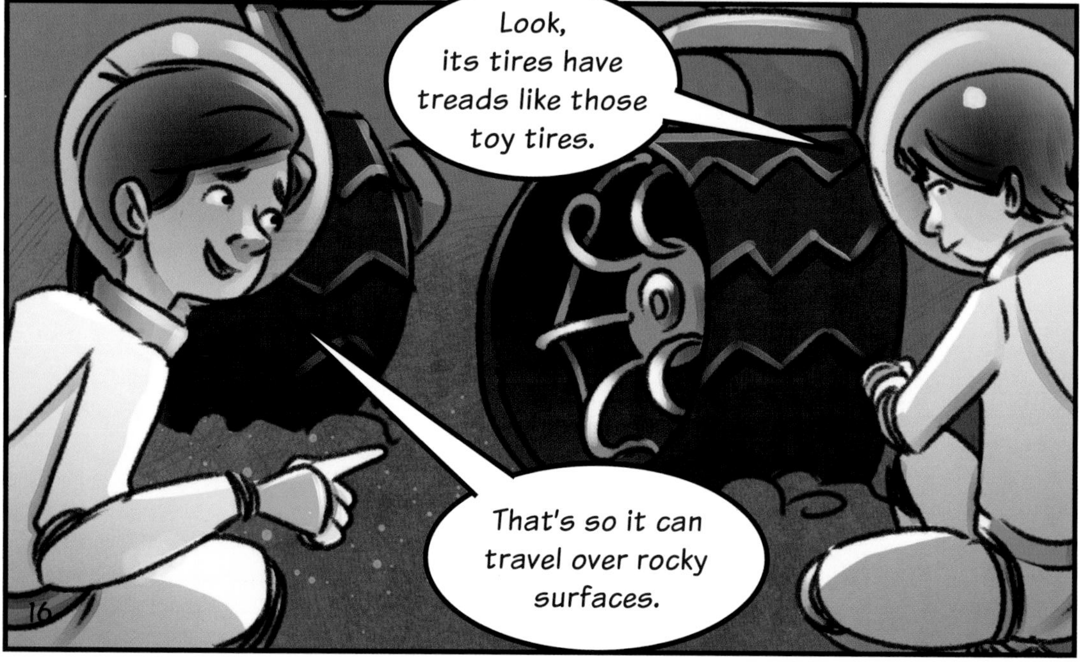
Look, its tires have treads like those toy tires.
That's so it can travel over rocky surfaces.

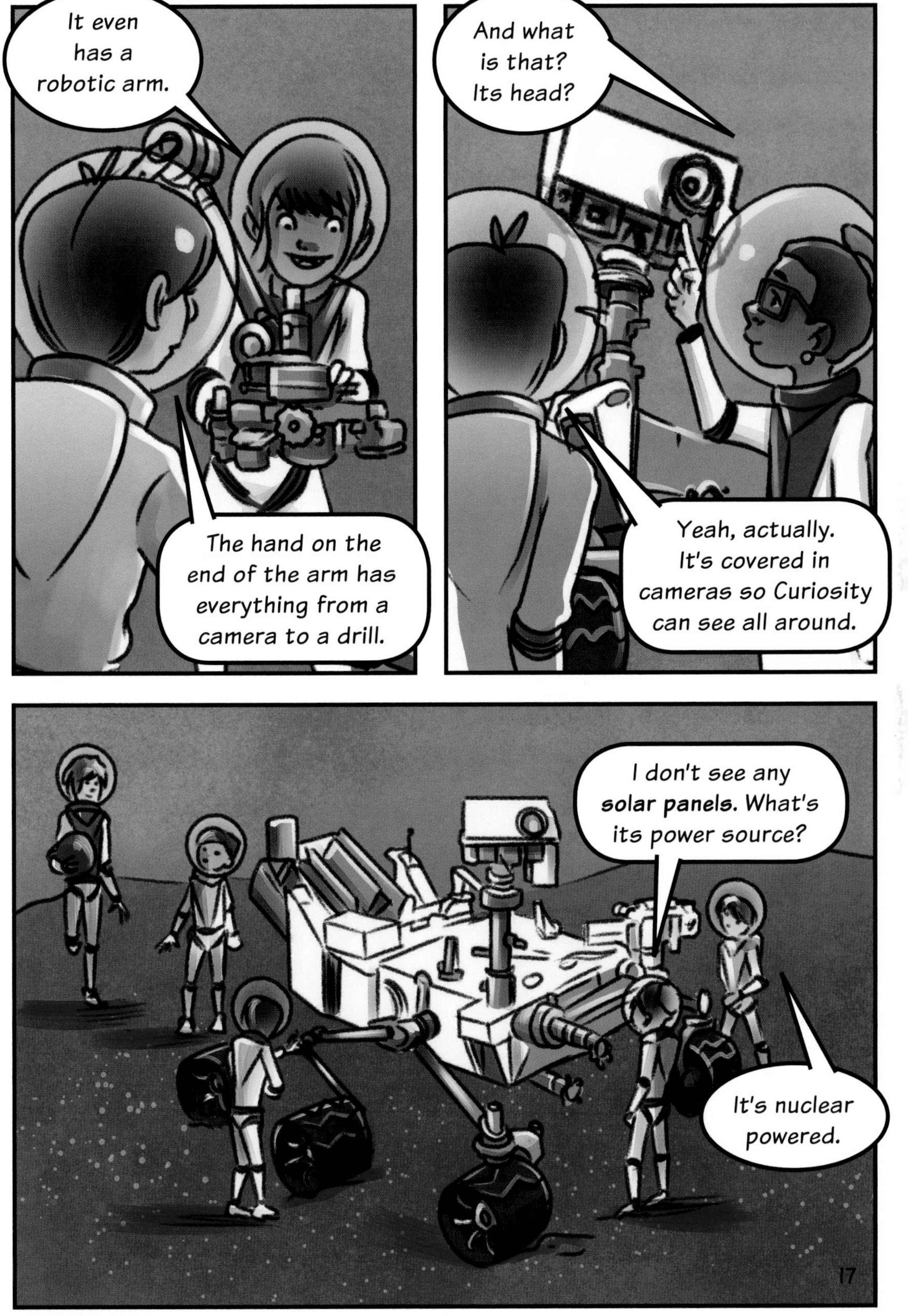
It even has a robotic arm.
The hand on the end of the arm has everything from a camera to a drill.
And what is that? Its head?
Yeah, actually. It's covered in cameras so Curiosity can see all around.
I don't see any **solar panels**. What's its power source?
It's nuclear powered.

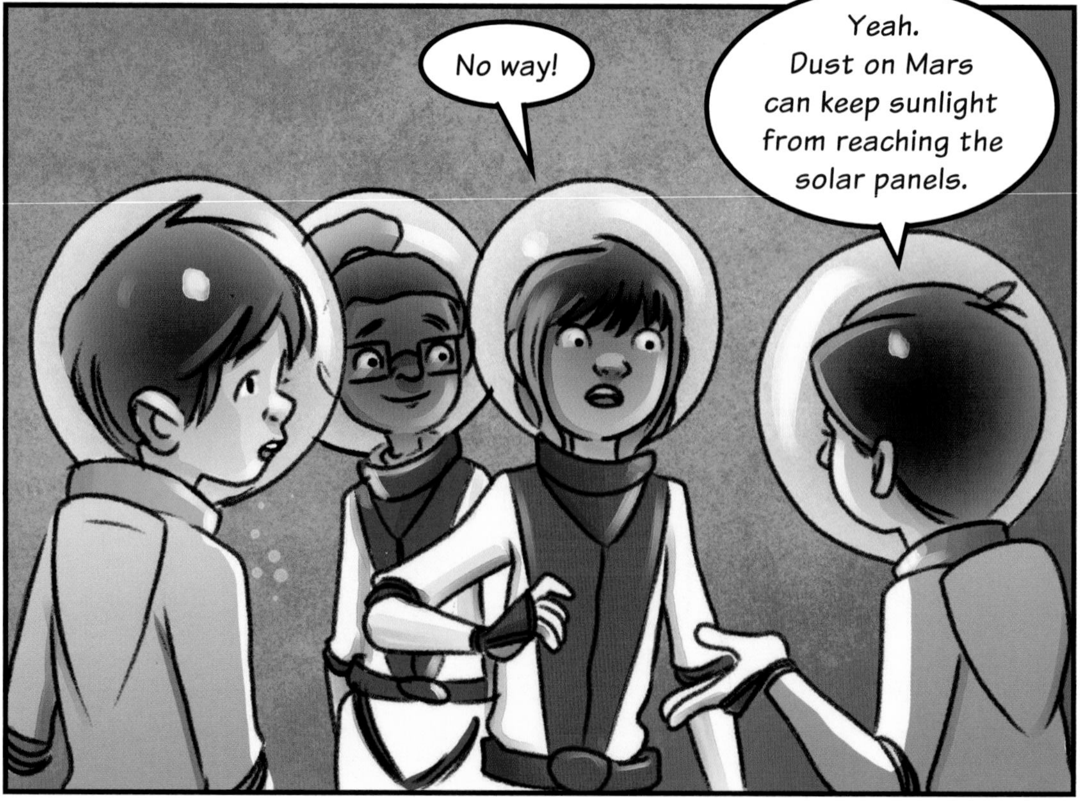
No way!
Yeah. Dust on Mars can keep sunlight from reaching the solar panels.

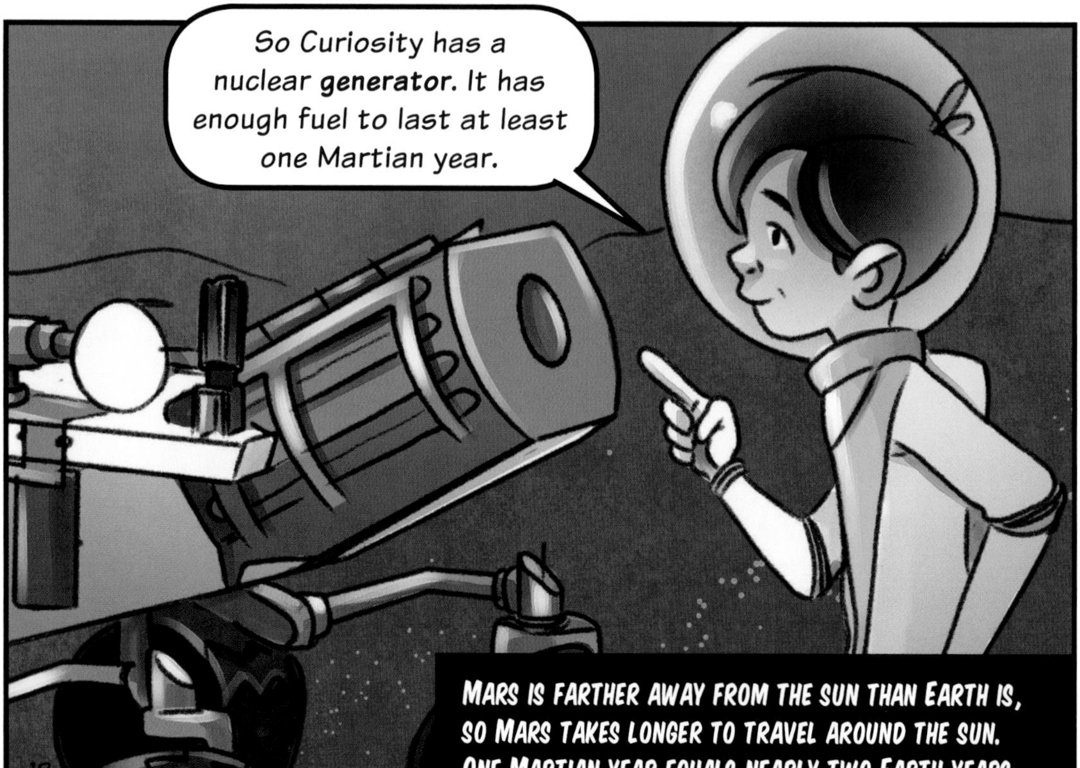
So Curiosity has a nuclear **generator**. It has enough fuel to last at least one Martian year.
MARS IS FARTHER AWAY FROM THE SUN THAN EARTH IS, SO MARS TAKES LONGER TO TRAVEL AROUND THE SUN. ONE MARTIAN YEAR EQUALS NEARLY TWO EARTH YEARS.

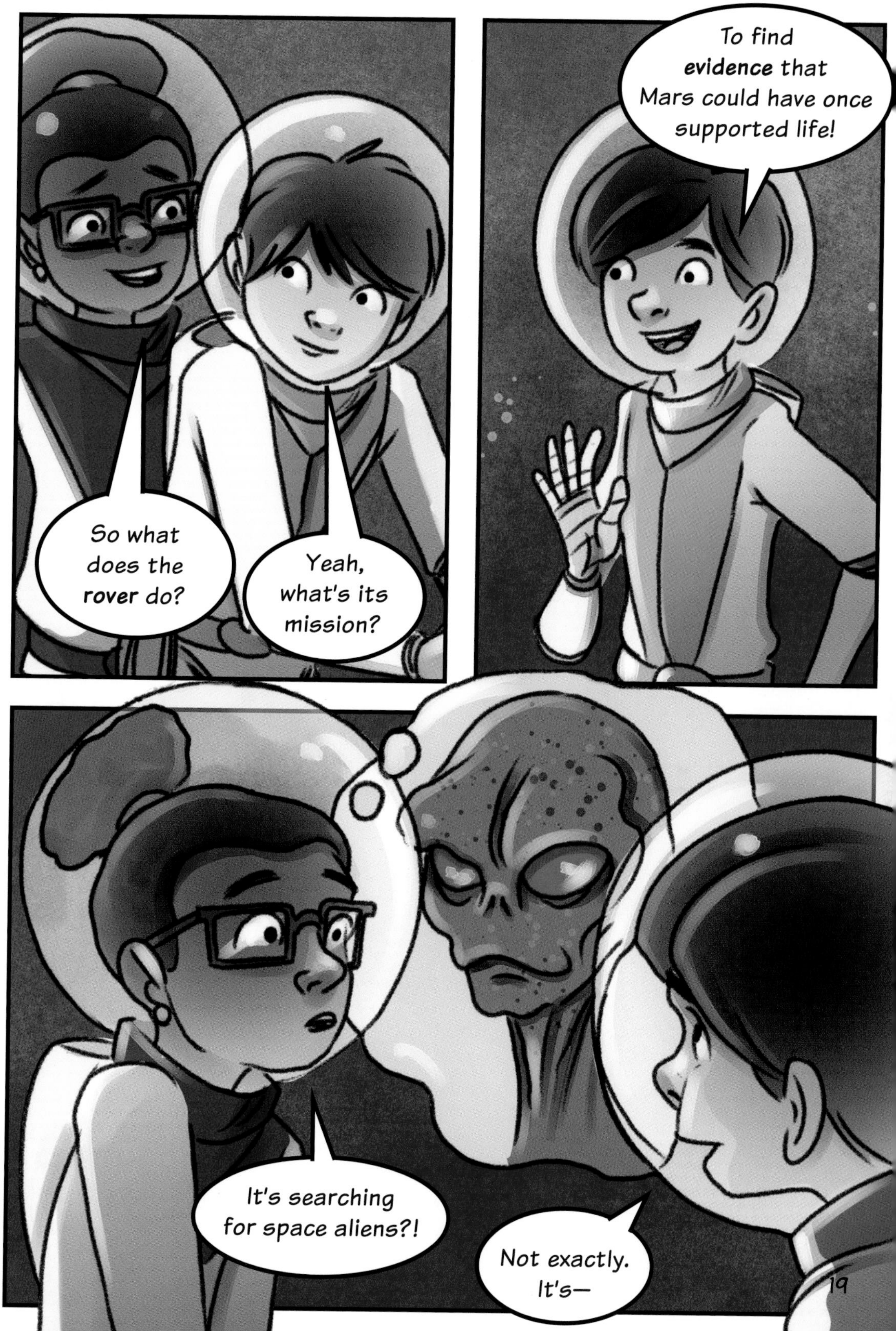

So what does the **rover** do?
Yeah, what's its mission?
To find **evidence** that Mars could have once supported life!
It's searching for space aliens?!
Not exactly. It's—

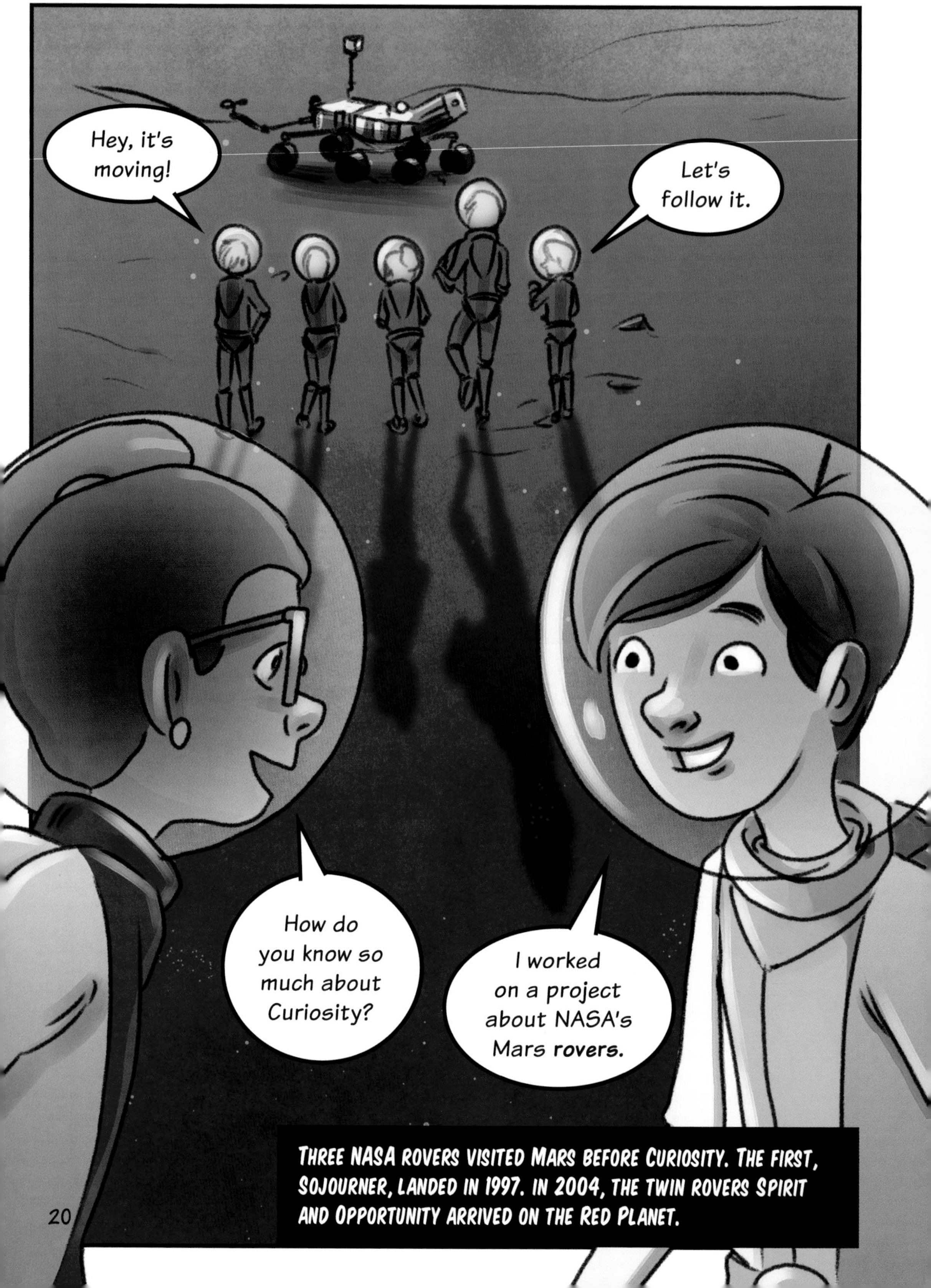
Hey, it's moving!
Let's follow it.
How do you know so much about Curiosity?
I worked on a project about NASA's Mars **rovers**.
THREE NASA ROVERS VISITED MARS BEFORE CURIOSITY. THE FIRST, SOJOURNER, LANDED IN 1997. IN 2004, THE TWIN ROVERS SPIRIT AND OPPORTUNITY ARRIVED ON THE RED PLANET.

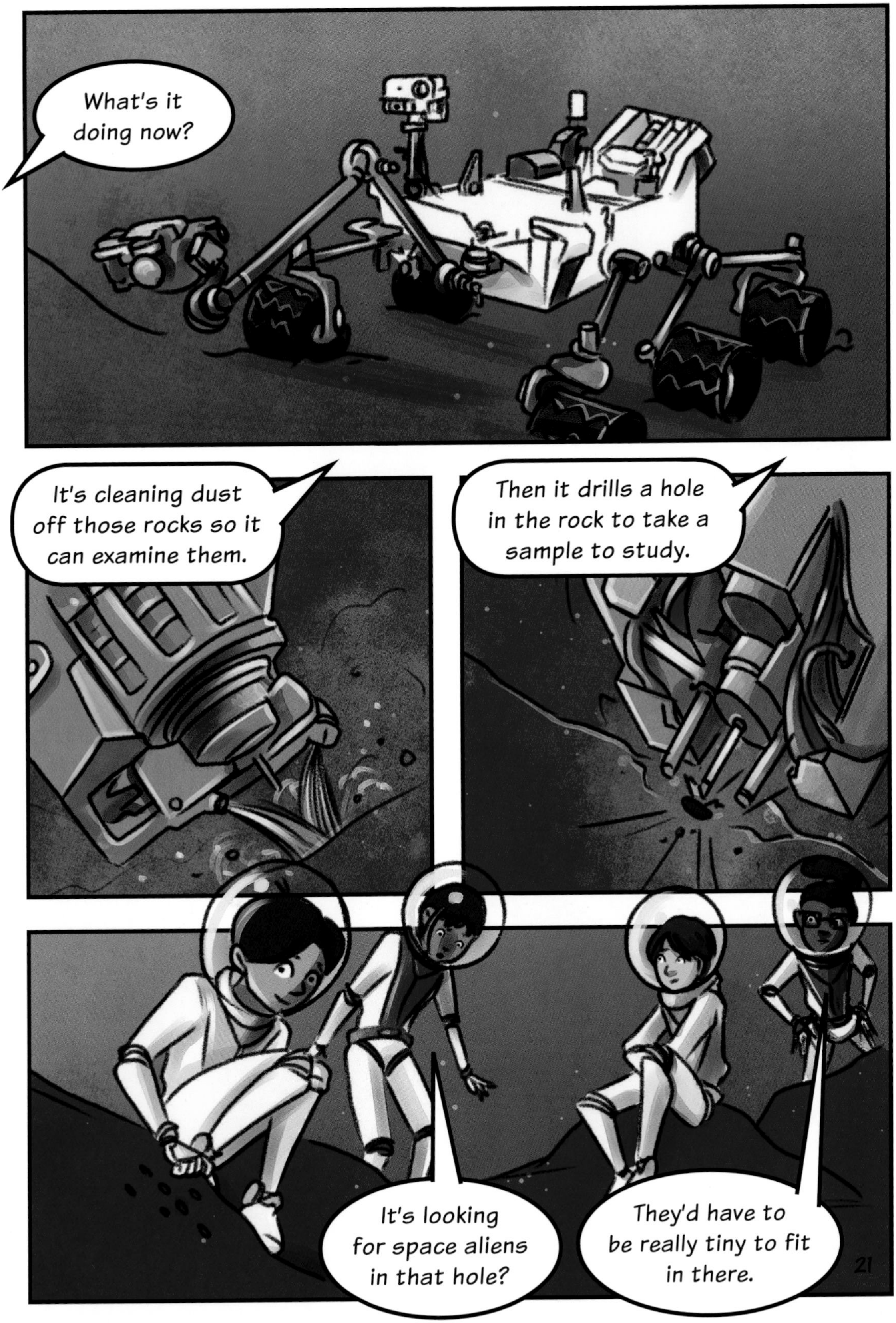
What's it doing now?
It's cleaning dust off those rocks so it can examine them.
Then it drills a hole in the rock to take a sample to study.
It's looking for space aliens in that hole?
They'd have to be really tiny to fit in there.

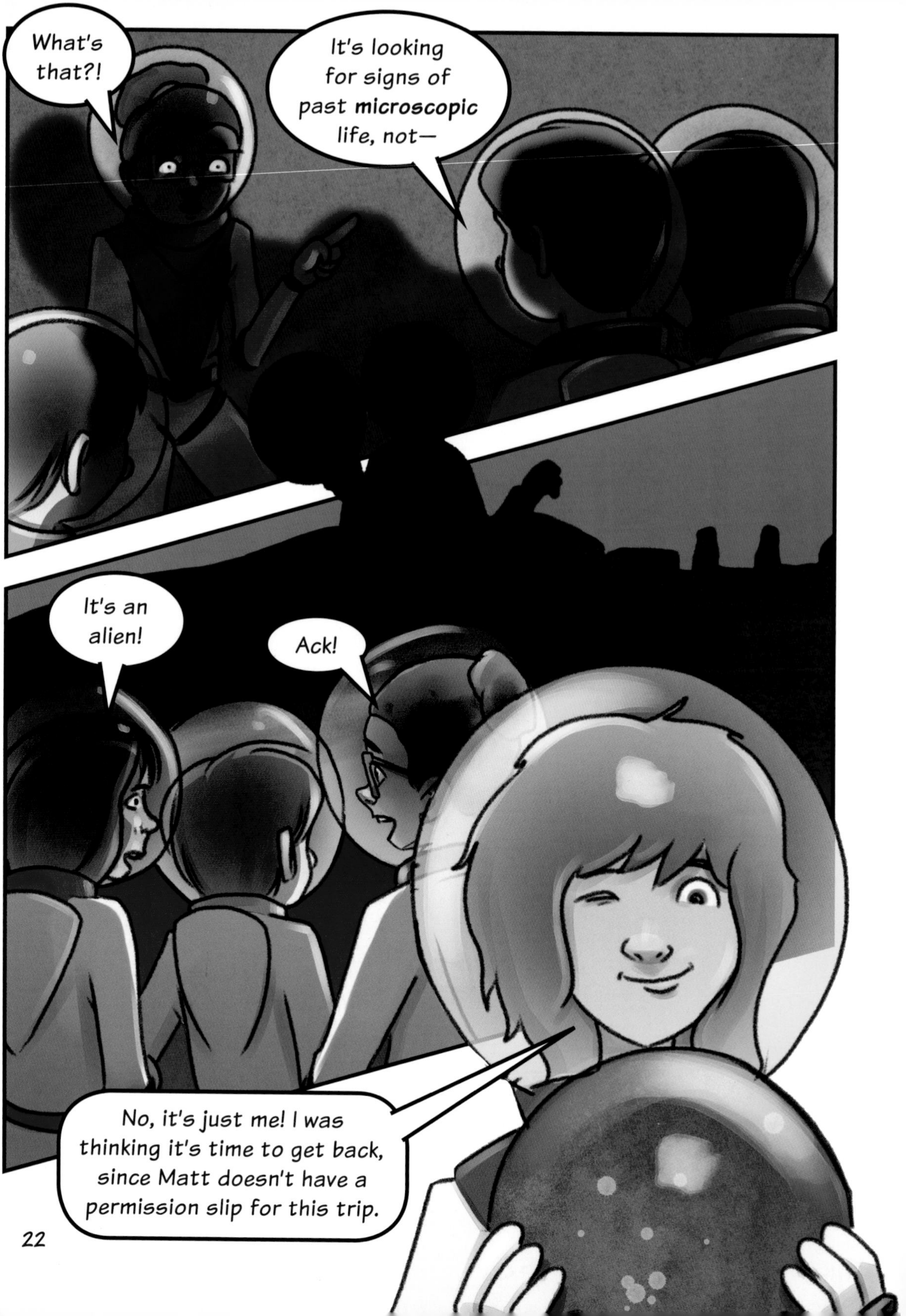
What's that?!
It's looking for signs of past **microscopic** life, not—
It's an alien!
Ack!
No, it's just me! I was thinking it's time to get back, since Matt doesn't have a permission slip for this trip.

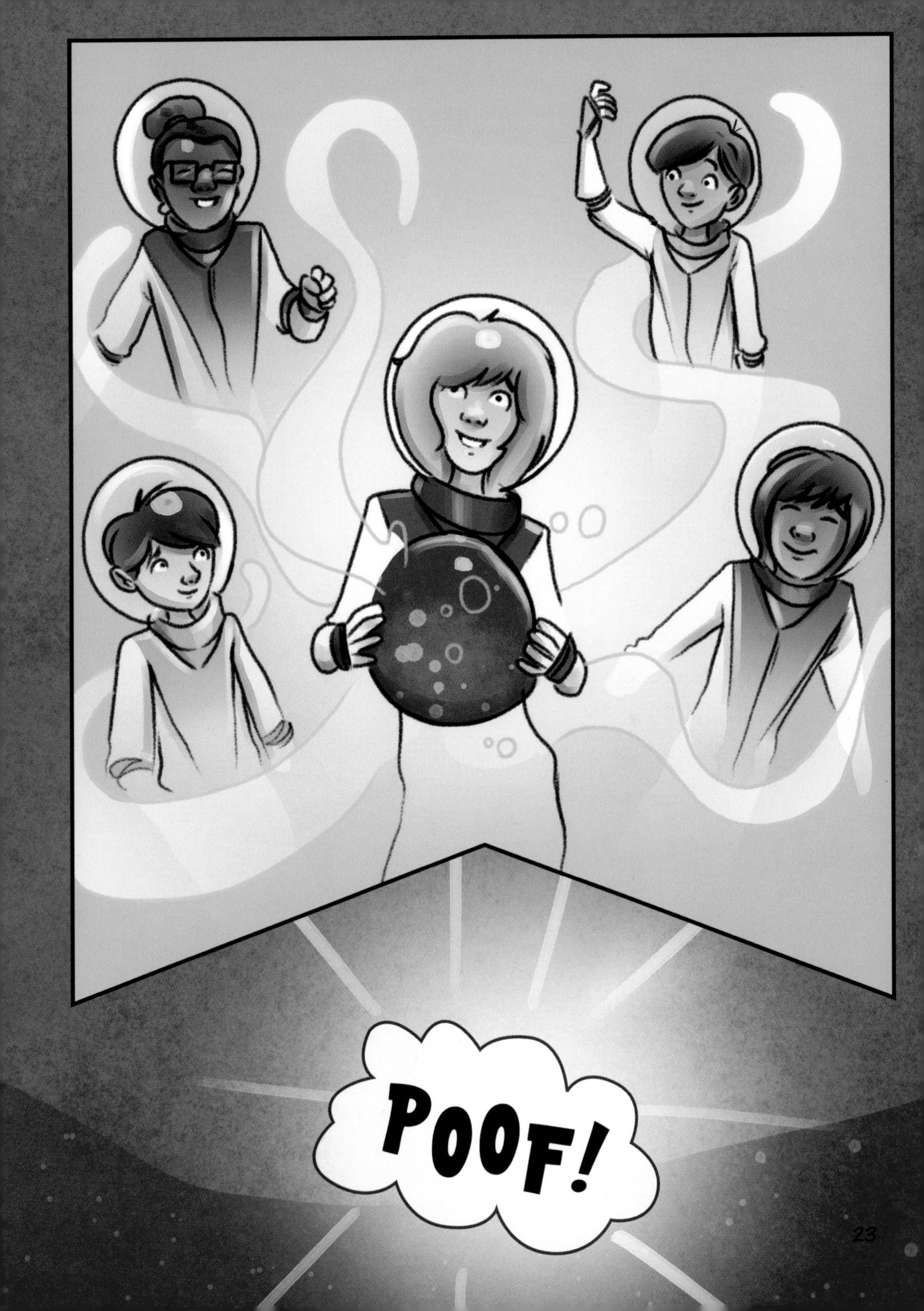
POOF!

THE ROVER

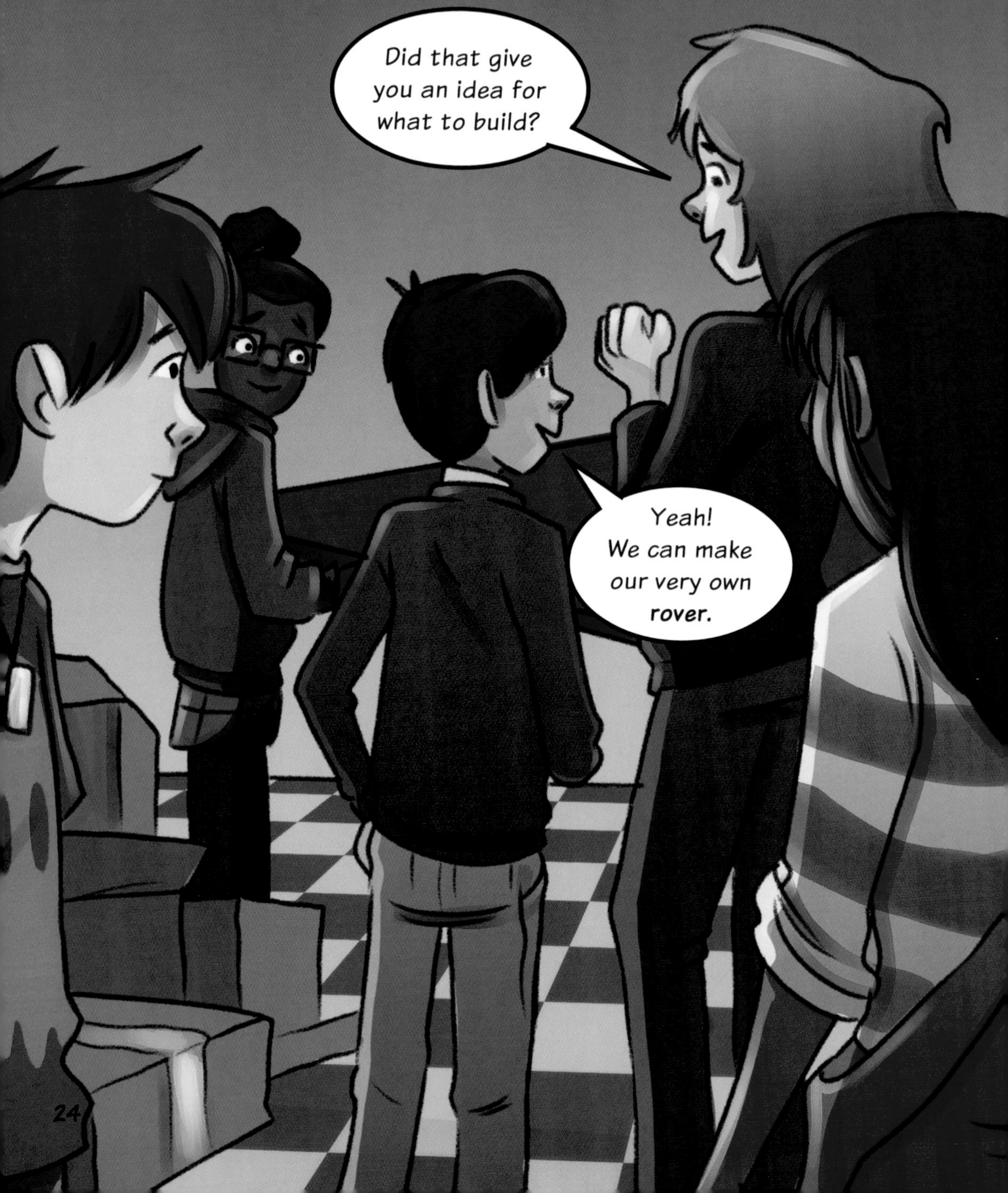
Did that give you an idea for what to build?
Yeah! We can make our very own **rover**.

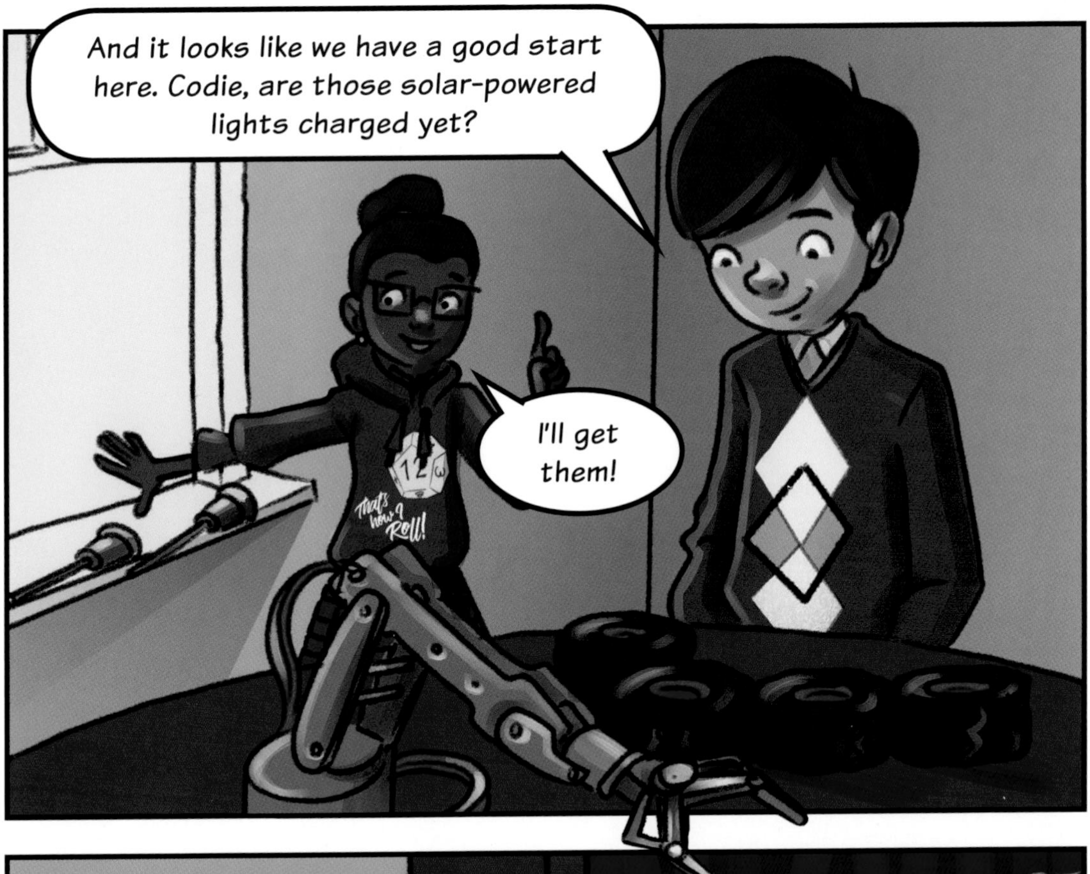
And it looks like we have a good start here. Codie, are those solar-powered lights charged yet?
I'll get them!

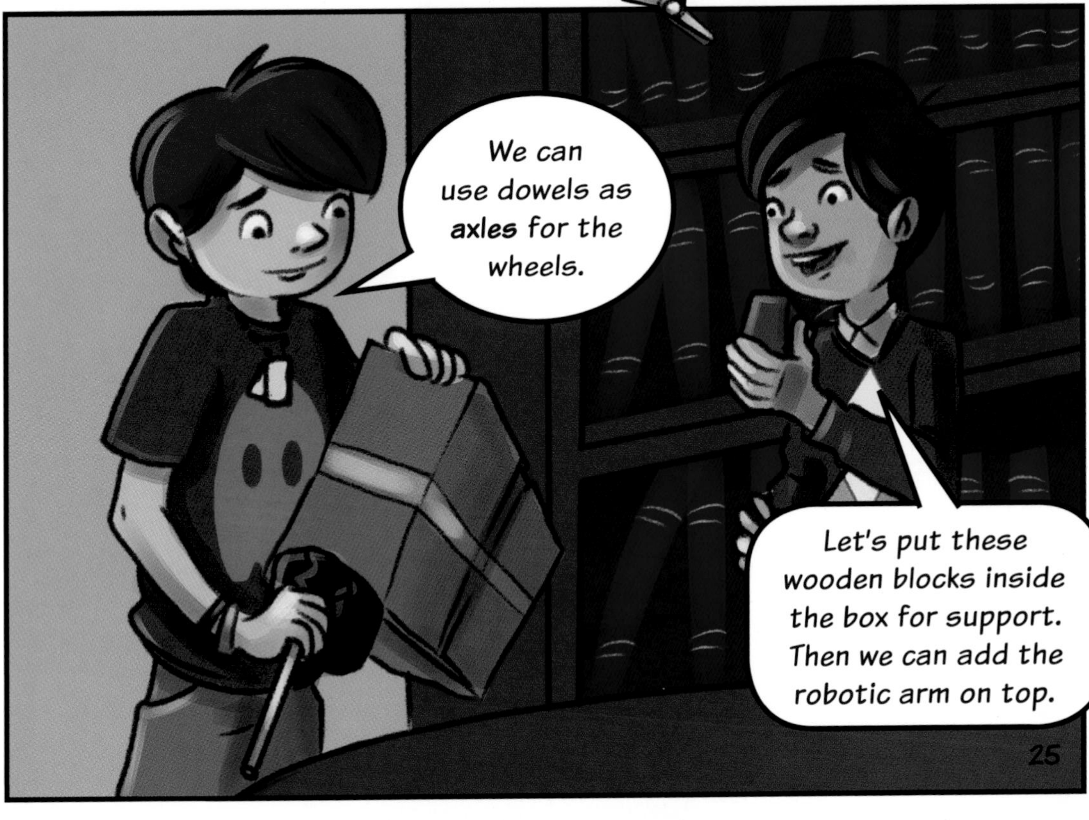
We can use dowels as **axles** for the wheels.
Let's put these wooden blocks inside the box for support. Then we can add the robotic arm on top.

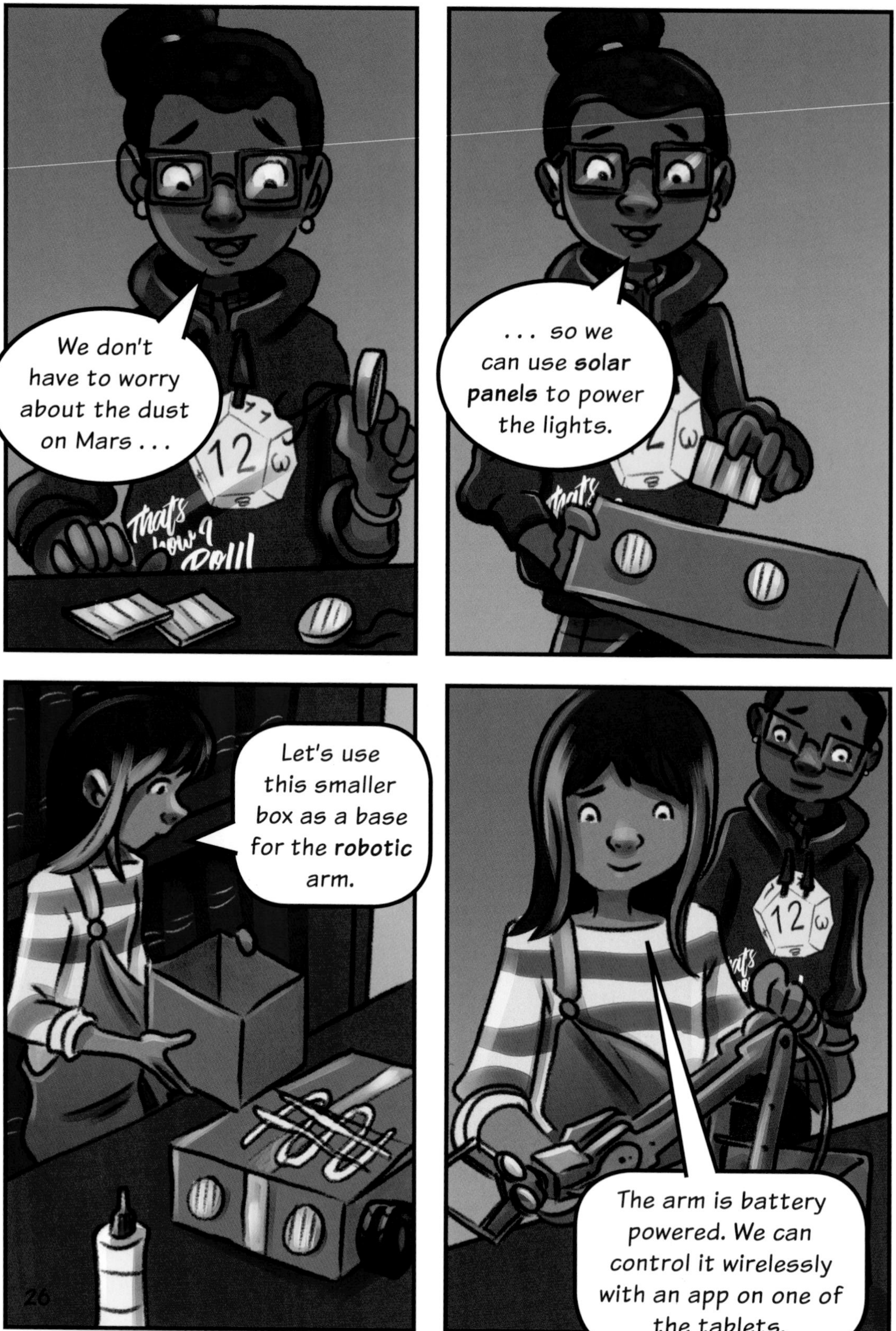
We don't have to worry about the dust on Mars . . .
. . . so we can use **solar panels** to power the lights.
Let's use this smaller box as a base for the **robotic** arm.
The arm is battery powered. We can control it wirelessly with an app on one of the tablets.

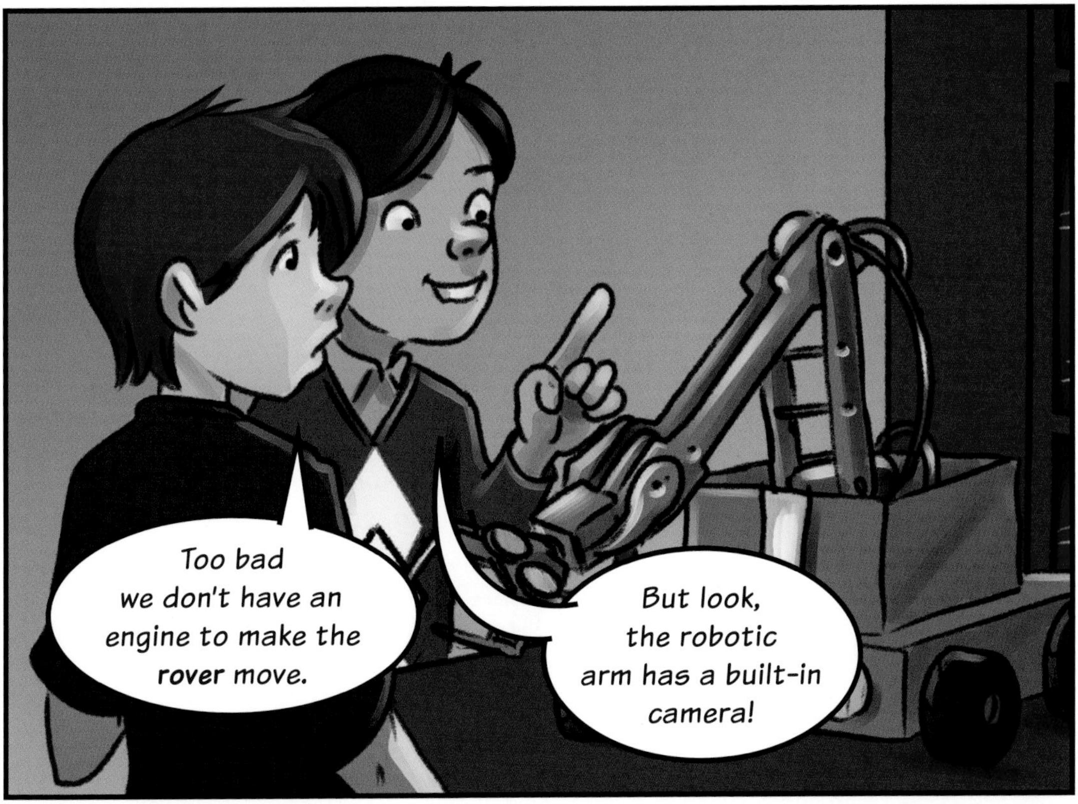
Too bad we don't have an engine to make the **rover** move.
But look, the robotic arm has a built-in camera!

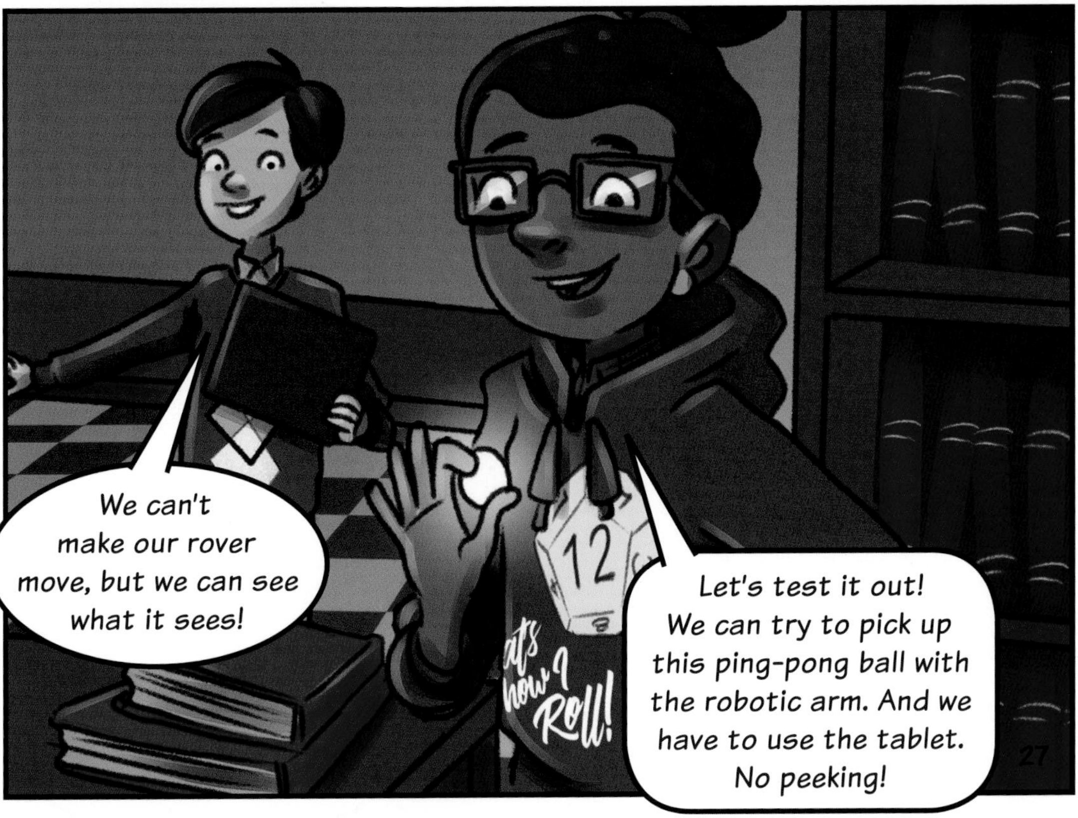
We can't make our rover move, but we can see what it sees!
Let's test it out! We can try to pick up this ping-pong ball with the robotic arm. And we have to use the tablet. No peeking!
12
That's how I Roll!

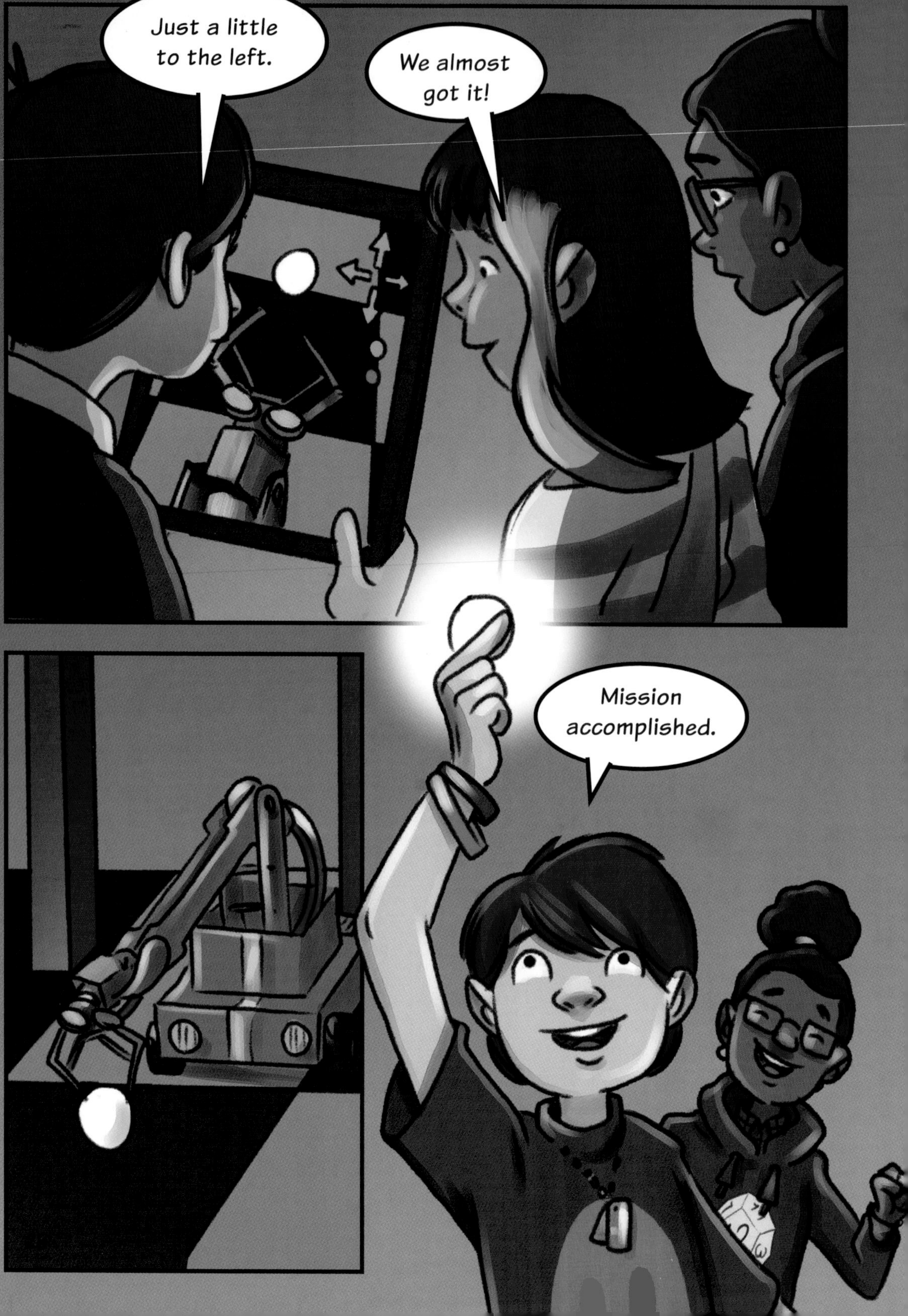
Just a little to the left.
We almost got it!
Mission accomplished.

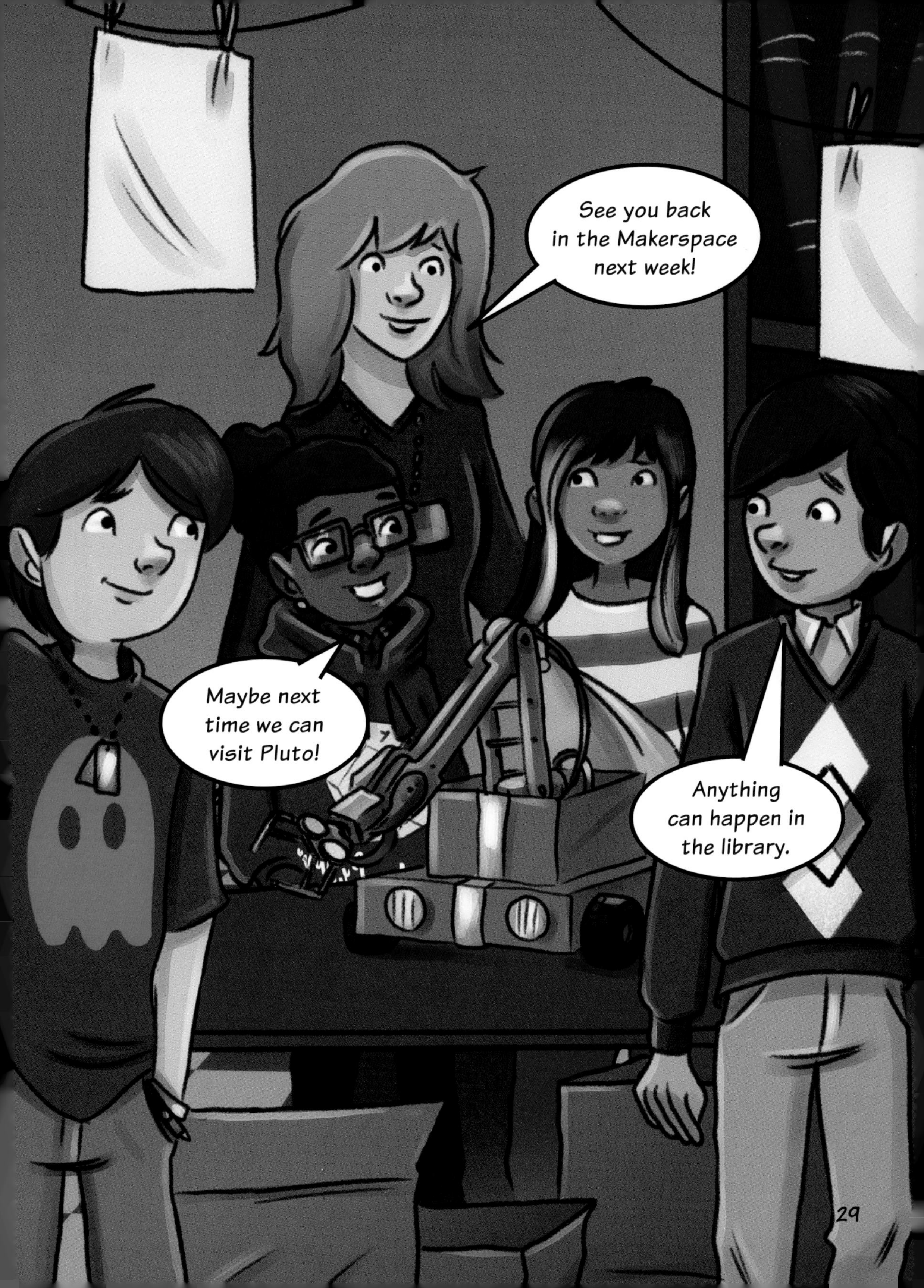
See you back in the Makerspace next week!
Maybe next time we can visit Pluto!
Anything can happen in the library.

GLOSSARY

axle—pole on which wheels revolve

evidence—signs that show something to be true

generator—machine that produces electricity

microscopic—so tiny that a microscope is needed to see it

rover—vehicle used for exploring

solar panels—group of cells designed to collect energy from the sun and turn it into electricity

CREATE YOUR OWN MAKERSPACE!

1. Find a place to store supplies. It could be a large area, like the space in this story. But it can also be a cart, bookshelf, or storage bin.

2. Make a list of supplies that you would like to have. Include items found in your recycling bin, such as cardboard boxes, tin cans, and plastic bottles (caps too!). Add art materials, household items such as rubber bands, paper clips, straws, and any other materials useful for planning, building, and creating.

3. Pass out your list to friends and parents. Ask them for help in gathering the materials.

4. It's time to create. Let your imagination run wild!

BUILD A ROBOT!

WHAT YOU NEED

• Cardboard boxes
• Various Makerspace items

Every robot has a mission, or a task it is designed to do. Rovers are used to explore, so they have wheels. Robots that are used to move objects have robotic arms. Other robots gather data, so they have radios and antennae to send information.

1. Imagine what you want your robot to do. Make of list of the different tasks.

2. Next to each task, list what the robot needs to complete the task. For example:

> Task 1: Explore faraway places — wheels
>
> Task 2: Pick up rock samples — arm with pincers

3. Search your Makerspace for items that might help your robot achieve its goal. If it needs to send information, use pipe cleaners for antennae. If your robot needs to move, make wheels out of paper plates or circles of cardboard. Grab markers to draw buttons and dials. Find pieces of paper for panel doors.

4. Using a cardboard box as a base, start building your robot!

FURTHER RESOURCES

Christopher, Nick. *Exploring Mars*. New York: KidHaven, 2018.

Furstinger, Nancy. *Robots in Space*. Minneapolis: Lerner, 2015.

Holzweiss, Kristina. *Amazing Makerspace DIY Basic Machines*. New York: Children's Press, 2017.

Miller, Shannon McClintock, and Blake Hoena. *A Coding Mission*. North Mankato, MN: Capstone, 2019.

Morey, Allan. *Mars Rovers*. Minneapolis: Bellwether Media, 2018.